NOTES FROM A DESERTER

A SOLDIER'S JOURNEY HOME

By C. W. Towarnicki

Notes from a Deserter © copyright 2025 Chad Towarnicki. All rights reserved. No part of this book may be reproduced in any form whatsoever, by photography or xerography or by any other means, by broadcast or transmission, by translation into any kind of language, nor by recording electronically or otherwise, without permission in writing from the author, except by a reviewer, who may quote brief passages in critical articles or reviews.

NO AI TRAINING: Without in any way limiting the author's exclusive rights under copyright, any use of this publication to "train" generative artificial intelligence (AI) technologies to generate text is expressly prohibited. All rights to license uses of this work for generative AI training and development of machine learning language models are reserved.

Chapter 11, "A Flimsy Gallows," was originally published in *Sundial Magazine.*

ISBNs: 978-1-963452-13-6 (pb);
978-1-963452-14-3 (eBook)

Book Cover Design: The Book Cover Whisperer, OpenBookDesign.biz
Interior Book Design: Inanna Arthen, inannaarthen.com

Library of Congress Control Number: 2024918810
First Printing: 2025
Printed in the United States of America

Names: Towarnicki, C.W., author.
Title: Notes from a deserter : a soldier's journey home / by C. W. Towarnicki.
Description: [Roseville, Minnesota] : HTF Publishing, [2025]
Identifiers: ISBN: 978-1-963452-13-6 (paperback) | 978-1-963452-14-3 (ebook)
Subjects: LCSH: Military deserters--Pennsylvania--History--19th century--Fiction. | Farmers-- Pennsylvania--History--19th century--Fiction. | Bounty hunters--United States--History-- 19th century--Fiction. | Soldiers--United States--Correspondence--Fiction. | War and society--Fiction. | United States--History--Civil War, 1861-1865--Fiction. | LCGFT: Historical fiction. | Linked stories. | BISAC: FICTION / Historical / General. | FICTION / Historical / Civil War Era. | FICTION / Short Stories.
Classification: LCC: PS3620.O9458 N68 2025 | DDC: 813/.6--dc23

TABLE OF CONTENTS

1: Leaving Home 4
2: Recruiting Philadelphia 16
3: Inflating the Intrepid 24
4: Soldiers and Patients 34
5: Photographing the Dead 46
6: Friends and Enemies 57
7: Soldier's Heart 70
8: Runaways 79
9: Perkiomenville Hotel 91
10. John Brown's Tavern 107
11: A Flimsy Gallows 123
12: Witnesses 133
13: Writing Home 143
Notes from the Author 155
Acknowledgments 166
About the Author 168

1

Leaving Home

The early glow of dawn merged with the light of a hovering moon, and blushing red clouds cast faint shadows over the open meadow beside the farmhouse. A barred owl called out in echo of herself, with only a rooster answering.

In that dim beginning of the day, William emerged from the wood line holding two rabbits hanging stiff by their feet in one hand, and the traps that he pulled in the other. He was a thin man with the hint of a beard. He walked with short, stiff strides as if carrying an invisible sack of feed at all times.

Stepping into the field, he looked uphill toward the stone farmhouse bathing broadside in the sunrise. The window where his wife may have been watching from was a golden mirror of the eastern sky. With a slight tilt of his head, the broad brim of his straw planter's hat cast his face in shadow.

The shortening of the days, the recent rains, and his evolving understanding of raising crops had yielded a disorganized patchwork of fields that had not yet produced their potential. He worked the whole growing season in the hopes that his family would be able to rely on the harvest while he was gone to the war. If winter lingered, they would need wild fare to sustain them. He knew this well and laid in bed at night hoarding imaginary food stores in the damp corners of a springhouse in his mind. Between this imaginary work and dreaming, he could never find the words to tell Hannah of his plans to enlist. Somehow, though, she already knew.

Leaving Home

They had come to this plot through Hannah and her father, Charles. Her dowry was significant, and Charles contributed what his son-in-law could not. These negotiations had taken place inside their future home, at their future table, with Charles leading the discussion and William sitting outside on the porch. From that vantage point, he could see the potential of the property, but he had much to learn.

William now approached the two outbuildings that represented his education in carpentry. The first, a small tool shed, looked as though it would not survive the next winter. It slouched more into the soft soil with every rainfall. Its companion, a much larger and sturdier success by comparison, stored the primary ploughs and farming equipment, with an overhung stable to protect the two mules from the weather. They were barrels with legs, knock-kneed but dependable, indifferent to him moving about in and around the barn.

He splayed and skinned the rabbits at a thin workbench. After placing each mouthful of meat in a wooden bowl, he pulled the two thin hides over fur stretchers and hooked them under the brim of the overhang. Wiping his hands clean of blood and fur, he stowed the last of his traps away. He paused at the base of the ladder to the hay loft, feeling the rungs sanded smooth from usage. In the loft above he sat amidst plumes of dust and stale air splintered in bars by the morning light.

In this quiet place, the world around him settled back into a still sleep. She would not understand his reasoning for leaving. "It's not my father's farm," she would say again. "It's ours. He helped in what way he could." The same couched phrases that ran through his head in the fields and made him feel like a sharecropper on his own land. To be a soldier was something greater than a farmer; to risk one's life for the land rather than giving one's life to it.

He was born into the Hauck family but believed in an American future for his offspring more than a German past. When he married, he sought to change the spelling of the surname to Howe, becoming the deep-rooted trunk of a new family tree that would one day spread well beyond his personal proving grounds of these few fields with fruit trees turning orange-leaved in July.

Their firstborn, a son, was named after Charles. William hoped the second would be another boychild, to be named after himself. Working the land that Charles had paid for, living in the house that Hannah had selected, William would have to accomplish something on his own for his eponymous gift to carry any value as the Howe family sapling began to branch.

Through the rough-cut window in the loft, the rising tide of sunlight on the ground had reached the far stone wall of the property. A large granite boulder that marked the property at the roadside turned its shoulder up in the light and tucked its head down and away into the cool darkness that hung in the woods. The stores of food were substantial. The variety of animals were well fenced and housed. While he was gone, he could write to her, a discharged soldier had explained one night at the local Perkiomenville Hotel. "Now, I wasn't writing my family every week," he had said, "but there is a lot of downtime if you need a way of getting into a local town to find a postmaster."

William hesitated to respond. "I'm not sure I can do it. She'll be having a baby this winter. She can't start the growing season with the infant."

"You know what? I'll give you the honest truth." The soldier glared at William. "Plenty others have figured it out." He stood and in doing so revealed to William that they were not only similar in age but also similar in build. "This war has dragged on so long; I can't imagine it lasting six months more. How much longer can it go?"

William considered the man's words knowing full well he had already made up his mind. Looking around the tavern through the cigar-laden haze he saw very few men in their early 20s. The older famers barked and laughed at one another sharing clumsy gossip and debating prices for the harvest season.

The soldier added, "I'd imagine that if she cares at all about the union, then she'll understand."

And yet William knew Hannah's focus was only their small family. From the window of the hay loft he peered out to the farmhouse to discern if anyone was yet stirring. A great blue heron was in flight, glowing red in the sunrise, crossing clouds and croaking as it went.

He produced a small booklet and a worn pencil. With quiet concentration, he peeled single shavings from the tip of the pencil with a penknife. The booklet was slightly larger than his hand, leather bound with faded yellow pages, half filled with rough measurements and unfinished thoughts in diagram. He was out of practice with his handwriting, yet he began drafting the words he had not been able to say.

He touched the tip of the pencil to his tongue and began: *I worried over telling you for weeks. I only want what's best. I'll write you.* The letter was labored over yet primitive; short phrases straining and buckling under their message.

He paused, itching the straw away from his leg. One of the mules crossed the view of the window and the other followed. They headed toward the light in the field. The granite boulder was now glowing white.

I aim to be back before the baby is born. "December", he said to himself in a whisper. Tucking the booklet into his chest pocket, he looked around the barn as if he were seeing it for the first time or the last, then descended the ladder.

William filled two pails from the pump at the base of a massive black walnut trunk supporting two gnarled limbs that held their knots and burls up and out. He cranked the buckets down one at a time. *Every day's a bucket,* he thought. He laughed to himself, and his breath rose in visible wisps. The air was growing colder with each morning. He hoisted a full bucket onto the lip of the well.

When he had filled both pails, he leaned his chest against the stone ring and let a rock fall from his hand. He watched the ripples kick up light and settle back into the darkness.

"Plenty deep," he said.

He released a larger stone, which stirred the well again.

"Water. That's about all that I know for sure. We've got water."

The worn state of the ropes and buckets assured him after a tug that they would withstand the change in season.

The mules stirred. They kicked up doves that had huddled in the sun, and as William watched them rise, he could sense his wife looking out one of the second story windows. She would be up by now, and likely their son, looking out at the sunrise and the weather. A few more tugs on the well rope were to assure her, if she was watching, of what he already knew. *Everything's been left in working order.*

William toted the water to the back door of the house trying now to breathe patterns into the air. He did not worry over marching or camp life, indeed it was not far off from his preferred back country way of life. He was known for his marksmanship, and so he had naive over-confidence for when he might need to raise an arm. He returned to the outbuildings once more to retrieve the bowl of rabbit and a small basket where he had placed a few chicken eggs the day before. He counted seven eggs and made his way inside for breakfast to face what had become his greatest fear.

Hannah was cradling a small toddler with one arm and directing a poker at the logs in the fireplace with the other. Her brown hair hung tangled, tied up in the back like an abandoned nest. William had started the fire in the dark.

"Morning," he said as he filled a large cauldron that hung over the fire. The second pail was set aside for drinking water.

Raking the coals into a flat, even pile, he placed a grate over the rising flames with two cast iron pans. He emptied the rabbit meat into one and, kneeling low, he broke the eggs into the other.

His eyes watered ever-so-slightly as he studied the eggs simmering in the pan. "How are you feeling?"

Hannah stood behind him, rocking young Charles with both arms now, as he rode the rise of her belly. Her gaze was fixed on the baby's face, as if she had not heard William at all.

"I'm a little nauseous," she said. "I'm fine. This little one's got a fever that I can't help him break."

When Hannah and her father had negotiated the purchase of the farmstead, Hannah had not known then that she was already pregnant. William would have to learn the labor of farming and fatherhood simultaneously. Over the period of a few years, he was able to cut down a meadow and turn it over into several different crops. A flattened patch of earth was manicured into a small orchard. The land offered what he was willing to earn from it, and now with him leaving he worried how it might call in a debt. Hannah's father owned it, and lived nearby, but it was William who strained to bring it to life. Short, stiff strides from one corner of the fields to the other, rain or shine, wanting to make something of his own that his children could take pride in. When that dream lost its momentum, he turned to the idea of enlisting.

Hannah lifted the baby up and held him out in front of her at eye level, her belly picking up the front of her dress. "He's just burning up."

She draped Charles against her shoulder as she exited the room, returning with a loaf of bread.

"When did you bake this?"

"While you were down the river yesterday." She placed it on the table without eye contact. "What all did you catch? You were gone quite a while."

William picked up his son and carried him to the highchair at the table.

He struggled to put it into words for her. He worried that she would feel abandoned—worried more that they would get along fine without him. The neighbors were kind and beckoned to each other with their cast iron bells in times of need and times of plenty. Her family would swarm with the birth of the second child, just as they had with the first. He had whittled his temporary absence down to being inconsequential; it was the risk of a permanent departure that kept the words from forming in his mouth.

"Well," she said. "Were you even at the river?"

The pans sizzled and steamed. He removed them from the flame.

"Bill, you ain't fooling me."

He placed helpings on each plate, pushed Charles's chair closer to the table, and ate his share straight from the skillet as he stood between the fireplace and the door.

"I know you were at the courthouse."

The pressure of her gaze squeezed an awkward grin out of him.

"Bill, you can't go. I need you here. What sort of soldier would you make, anyway? You might be a good shot at a squirrel, but we both know that is not the same as killing a man."

William wiped the skillet with the broken end of the loaf and paused for a moment. He exhaled through his nose while chewing. Charles gripped and released a stuffed doll of a soldier at table, squeezed it tight in his grip, then dropped it again.

"I'm going, Hannah," he said without looking up. "I'm heading to Philadelphia tomorrow. It's something I've got to do." He filled his mouth with the egg-soaked bread to delay his next response.

Leaving Home

For a moment, it was as if nothing had changed. Charles now swinging the stuffed doll against the edge of the table, the wooden head knocking. William was standing and chewing with the skillet still warm in his hand. A damp log in the fire popped and rolled over with a hiss.

The toddler sensed the stillness and began to cry but neither parent moved.

William could only shrug to himself, punctuating his admission. "I've worried over telling you for weeks," he said. "Weeks, now. They are offering as much as sixteen dollars a month."

Seeing his mother in distress, Charles now began to writhe in his highchair.

"It'll only be three months' time. I aim to be back before the baby comes. Most people don't think this war will last much longer—"

Her plate struck William high in the chest, and she pounded up the stairs clutching her son who squeezed the soldier doll tight.

Outside, William mustered up an extended dialogue with Hannah while she remained inside, upstairs. He rounded up both mules, yoked them together, and set out to pull what ears of corn were ready for storage.

He hitched the two mules to a small wagon, hardly bigger than a wheelbarrow, which could fit only a few boxes—a large one for corn and two smaller ones for any late berries or apples that had ripened. William kicked the mules up into a trot and they dragged the wagon like a sled through the mud. It was quick work filling the crates. From this far field it brought him comfort to see the property alive but mostly tamed, a quilt work of subsistence skirting the farmhouse perched on a hill. With a soldier's salary and name, their children would know this plot and this country was theirs.

11

Leaving the field, the mules struggled to drag the wagon back through the slough. The thin wooden wheels locked up and slid, creating deepening ruts. As he urged them to continue on, one mule bucked wildly, jolting the yoke and the wagon. Fighting to get to drier ground, it only worked itself and the wagon deeper.

"Get up," William said. "Get up. We're more than halfway there."

The calmer of the two took slow, patient steps, leaning away and sinking less. Eventually all three, man and mules, took to standing and testing the depth and density of the soil. The mules lifted their front hoofs, feeling the tug of the muck creating a seal. William poked a stick about, surveying the size and shape of the wallow.

He rocked the wagon forward and back, straining to torque the wagon free and failing. He paused for a moment, shook his head, scratched the back of his neck and recognized that he could hear the baby crying from afar—or was it a catbird? The wind was picking up and the sky above him had become one uniform layer of gray cloud that glowed with the light of the hidden sun. Again, he sensed Hannah watching.

Prodding with his fingers, he cleaned the muck out of the wheel spokes. He lodged a branch, about four feet in length, between the ground and the tail end of the wagon. With a flick of the reins, the mules began to pull. William pushed up on the branch. The wagon rocked up to the cusp of the ruts. The livelier mule, sensing firmer ground beneath her, kicked hard, twisting the yoke and the second mule backwards, wrenching the wagon firmly back into the mud. As the wagon tilted, William's branch lost pressure, and he was thrown onto his hands and knees in the soft, wet earth.

Under Hannah's watch, he left the mules and walked up to the larger outbuilding. There he retrieved two sets of panniers from the barn and returned to transfer the crops from the wagon to the packs on the mules. The calmer

LEAVING HOME

mule was the first to be unyoked, loaded up, and led to the main corral. The second remained tethered to the bogged-down cart.

A cold drizzle started as William marched back for the second mule. After loading the mule with the crops, it refused to move. William tugged at the reins, calling, "Come on. Get. Get." The mule was unflinching.

He dropped the reins, circled round the animal, placed his hands on its hindquarters and pushed. Snorting and shaking like a dog in the rain, the mule planted four hooves in the mud and tilted its head to see what the commotion was behind it.

William relaxed against frustration. He leaned on the animal to peer at the window where Hannah may have been. He saw only reflected panes of a gray sky. *I am going,* he thought. *This is something I've got to do. The children have to know I've made something for them.*

All at once, the mule came to life. Low pulls and short steps quickened to a trot, freeing the wagon and knocking William into the slop once more. He watched from his knees as the runaway mule sought its companion in the corral, wagon and all.

On the morning of his departure William pulled Charles from the crib at daybreak and carried him downstairs, shuffling his feet to keep the floorboards from creaking. He took up a page that had been torn from his notepad and folded once. He opened it and read it in murmurs to the baby before tucking it into the egg basket on the table.

He carried Charles down along the far fields to where a creek trickled across the property. Together they checked the muddy pass between the orchard and the crops where he had lain two boards to bridge the wallow. In the outbuildings, his tools were all tucked away and nearly two years' worth of firewood had been cut and stacked beside them. The baby caught a shiver in the springhouse where

William checked the store of meat and fish. As he climbed out, low sunlight was casting tall shadows that reached out into the fields in columns.

The coop had been lined a month early with hay for the coming cold. The baby tracked the hens as they rushed out into the yard and scattered. William gathered enough eggs for breakfast, dropped them in his coat pockets and carried his son inside.

Hannah was on her knees stoking the fire. She didn't look up as William entered the room, and he watched as she wrung her lips together and tended to the kindling.

The moment settled around them as they sat and ate their breakfast.

He could barely see his wife at the other end of the table—the light spilled through the window wrapping around her and pressing his eyes away.

"I haven't been looking forward to it," he said.

The baby bobbed up and down on his knee.

"You know they offer good pay," he said.

Hannah's breathing was deep. She never looked up.

He sat silent with one arm wrapped around the baby, his other hand flat on the table where the steam rose from his untouched food.

"December," William said, and took up his fork. "I'll be back in time for the baby."

He shared the full list of preparations. As Hannah listened, her face took on the blank resignation of a widow.

She remained at the table as William retrieved a small bag with a spare set of clothing, a heavy coat, and a canvas tarp to be used as a tent. As he said goodbye it was no bigger ceremony than leaving for town. He hugged Charles, nuzzled his warm cheek, and dropped a kiss on Hannah's head with his hand pressing on her belly.

Before leaving, he climbed up the shoulder of the granite boulder at the roadside. The windowpanes hung reflecting portraits of the sunrise. He held his hand up to Hannah, if she were watching, and whistled to the mules with no acknowledgment. After one last survey of his Perkiomenville farm, he started off on foot to the city of Philadelphia some thirty-five miles away.

2

RECRUITING PHILADELPHIA

In a hall that had been emptied and poorly furnished, an enlistment office was proving to be big business in Philadelphia. The hall itself was a towering brick edifice, with tall lean windows that pinched the natural light into the building, hanging in dusty rectangular columns. Tables were scattered about, and the tall ceilings amplified the boot steps and shuffling, the knocking, the hollering and calling of names. The volunteers herded into the building like cattle at feed time, only to exit out the other end looking somewhat the part of the soldier, dressed in blue and equipped with arms.

Mr. Morrow stood tall, nearly six and a half feet, and in the dust and the shuffling he moved with precision through the tangle of young men around him in the manner of a heron in a marsh. He would shepherd the men along, "Lines, boys. Lines. Won't make any sense of the lot of you unless we're in some semblance of order." The tobacco in his bottom lip urged him to suck against his teeth.

The volunteers were filtered toward Morrow, with his disheveled red hair crowning his lean frame. By his side, seated at their table, was Robert Young. His sharp blue eyes gleamed from his too fat face. Young tilted his head back to peer through circular glasses perched on the end of his nose.

At the enlistment office, they were the conduit through which a citizen would become a soldier. Some boys came through nervous as hell, some with the makings of honor, but Mr. Morrow handled them all the same. And on this day, near the end of August 1863, he was feeling fatigued by the ongoing war and the lack of suitable soldiers to send to it. In between volunteers he would say to his colleague phrases like "Mr. Young, I have my concerns", and "What are we sending them, Robert?"

Young would document their height, weight, age, and location of origin. Mr. Morrow would inspect their teeth and put them through a small battery of physical tests that included leaping vertically into the air, running in place, or receiving a strong thump on the chest or back. If a man passed, he'd be sent to the back of the factory, where they'd further document specifics about him, so the payment would be correct if he lived, or, if he died. A man could leave this hall in an hour or so, fully equipped with a musket and some version of the Union Blues. This was the product of the factory.

"Next!" Mr. Morrow would call, and another man would step up in a long line that wrapped along the inside wall and out the door, down the outside wall and up the block. The army needed able bodies that were bated with bills that read *To Arms, to Arms* and promises of a three-dollar premium added on to the first month's pay. Before entering the recruitment process, it was easy to convince oneself that $20 or more would be in hand before leaving the state.

"Next!" Mr. Morrow called, and a young boy stepped up.

He was small, even for his teenage years. His thin arms originated from skeletal shoulders, and he appeared covered in a sooty layer of dirt.

"Boy, what's about your age?" Mr. Morrow bent over him like a crane. The boy looked up to meet his eyes.

"I'm fifteen, sir."

"Oh, the hell you are, boy. Now, I'm going to ask you again, and if you lie to me, you can head right on out that door with a strong pat on the ass. Now, how old are you?"

He swept his dusty brown hair out of his face and said, "Sir, I'm thirteen."

"Thirteen, you say."

"Yes, sir."

As Young took the boy's height and weight down, Mr. Morrow took a few steps around the boy.

"You play the snare or the bugle?"

"I can play the snare."

"Now, where'd a farm boy like you get a snare?"

"We have one at home, sir. My father bought it when he was here in the city."

"And where's your father now?"

"We think he was killed in service, sir." His tone was a matter of fact. "Haven't heard from him in quite a while."

"You head on to the next section." Mr. Morrow pointed to the back corner of the great room, where a number of instruments and sheets of music were laid out on a table for impromptu serenades.

"No, sir."

Mr. Morrow bent down again, turning his ear to the boy. "Sorry?"

"I'd rather not drum. I want to serve the Union. I'm a crack shot."

Mr. Morrow took a deep breath and straightened out his frame, arching his back.

His dark eyes were deep-set in a pale face, and when he furrowed his brow, it cast a shadow that made his eye sockets appear bruised. He tucked his left hand up under his armpit and rested his right elbow overtop, while his thumb and forefinger tugged at the chaw in his lip.

"I appreciate the fervor, boy, but I can't. You head over there and show them you can play an instrument. That's your only chance."

"But sir. I'm determined to fight, I—"

"No, boy." Mr. Morrow tugged on the open flaps of his coat and straightened to his full height. "Now, if you get into the field and find your way to a gun, that'd be between you and the Lord—and I'd applaud it. Right here, though, your only chance of making it to the field is those instruments over there. Not another word."

The boy tilted his head in response, raising one eyebrow as he accepted. His head disappeared among the shoulders that crowded the line leading to Morrow and Young.

"Next, please, next!" Mr. Morrow called.

The man at the front of the line was in a daydream, looking off to where the boy had gone. The raps from the snare drum now caromed off the brick walls. In front of the instruments, men were being rough fitted for their uniforms. The enlistment officer beside them was finishing up a story, and the young men cackled and jeered at his punch line.

Arms were being distributed, along with supplies like canvas tents and canteens. The musket barrels poked and prodded the air as they exchanged hands, their hammers clapping shut as they were dry fired at a cloth dummy propped in the corner. Beneath the tall arching ceiling thick with clouds of unsettled dust and the murmur of conversation, the flutter of a pair of pigeons flown in through the open double doors shook the man from his trance.

"Next!" Mr. Morrow called again. "Are you next? Step up. Let's go." Mr. Morrow dug a wad of chaw from his lip and whipped it into a spittoon. He wiped his hand on his pants.

The man shrugged and stepped forward. "Yes, sir. Sorry."

He had a hint of a German accent that crept in despite his trying to bite down on it. He was another farmer sort. His hands and forearms looked akin to the hide of a horse, all muscle and veins under a brown coat of dust. He wore simple clothing and had a limp look about his face, where the moment had stolen away all expression. He removed his straw planter's hat, clutched it with both hands and spoke. "William H. Howe," he said, "of Perkiomenville."

Morrow grinned. "Quite the name. For both you

and your town. We'll have to get your hat replaced straight away." Glancing over Howe's shoulder, Mr. Morrow saw the crown of the young boy's head emerge from the crowd where firearms were being handed out.

"Sonofabitch! Young, do this one on your own."

Mr. Morrow caught the boy's attention as he waded over. The boy had gotten his hands on a musket, nearly his height in length. He yanked it from the boy's grasp.

"Dammit, boy. You aren't going armed." He turned to the officer distributing the guns. "He's not documented."

The boy offered no response other than a determined stare. As Mr. Morrow stood over him with the musket, the boy reached and grabbed the stock. He didn't pull it away from Mr. Morrow, he just held it.

Morrow studied the boy for a moment. His hands were small on the stock, with wrists as thin as kindling. He released the musket which was too barrel-heavy for the boy's grip. With both hands he wrenched against the weight of the gun, which tilted and clanked against the ground.

"You do what you want, boy. We've enough drummers already."

Mr. Morrow returned to his table, where Young was on to the next recruit.

"That boy is determined to fight, is he?" Young asked.

"Stubborn little bastard. That's for sure." Mr. Morrow reached into his pocket for a new pinch of chaw. Placing it in his lip, his speech was muffled. "How's that last one? Howe?"

"That farmer, there. He won't last a week. Say's he's a bit of a marksman but hasn't ever been outside of whatever back-country village he came from. Country boy. Wish I could give him a dose of what's in that boy's veins."

"They'll likely all bleed out the same, unfortunately." He leaned against the table and looked to the uniform tables. An officer dropped a hat onto the boy's head, and it slid forward over his eyes. The boy removed the hat quickly and tied a bandanna around his head. He replaced the hat with the proper fit. The size of the coat he was given would not be such an easy fix.

Mr. Morrow sighed into a yawn. He saw the farmer holding his musket, watching the undulating sea of men toss and turn from table to table. He looked abandoned, waiting for someone to return.

"Young, you might be right. That poor bastard is already exasperated. I'd hate to be marching on the Rebs with his sorry ass. I probably would take the boy."

Young shook his head in agreement, shuffled his papers and dipped his pen. Mr. Morrow wiped the drool from the corner of his lip.

"Next!"

Mr. Morrow looked to the front of the line where another thin individual was awaiting inspection. He leaned to Young and said, "Where're they hiding all the men?"

The recruit was taller, moving with the rigidity of a wooden figurine. Every motion, every step, every standing pose seemed overthought.

"Name?" Mr. Morrow asked.

"Francis Jack." His voice was both soft and high pitched.

"Frank Jack?"

"Well, I never went by Frank. I only go by Francis." He tugged the pitch of his voice into a lower register.

Mr. Morrow met Young's eyes. He sat, semi-reclined, inspecting the recruit. His pen was at the ready. He returned Mr. Morrow's gaze and gave him a soft nod.

"Could you please tell Mr. Young your height, weight, and age, Mr. Francis Jack?"

"I am 5' 10", 135 lbs, and I am eighteen years of age." Francis straightened his posture, tugging the ends of his coat down. It was a heavy coat that hid his slender frame. His delicate neck craned over the collar.

"Now let's have a look at you." Mr. Morrow circled the recruit. He snuck a raised eyebrow to Young. "Awful thick coat to wear on a warm day? Haven't you got one your size?"

"Want to be fit and ready for my first assignments."

Circling back to the table in front of the recruit, Mr. Morrow asked, "You're eighteen?"

"Eighteen years old, sir."

"Looks like you've never had to shave a day in your life."

"Shaved this very morning, sir."

Mr. Morrow flashed a knowing smile. His large hand perched on the recruit's shoulder, and he jostled him with a chuckle. Francis looked at Young for interpretation.

"Just shaved this morning, Francis Jack? Did we? Wanted to be ready for the enlistment officers?"

Francis shrugged. "I shave most mornings, sir."

Mr. Morrow's laughter amplified, and he shook Francis vigorously. "Do you now?"

He returned to his station beside Mr. Young, and Francis remained on display before him.

"Francis Jack. Mister Francis Jack." Mr. Morrow crossed his arms. "Are you ready to fight in this war?"

The recruit's face fell serious, with small red lips drawn tight and focused eyes. "I am," he said.

"Then you will."

Mr. Morrow gave him a slap in the back and pointed him towards the uniform distribution tables. "You're going to have to take that coat off to try on the blue coat, you know?"

"Thank you, Mr. Morrow." He reached out his hand, his wrist extending thin and pale from the hanging sleeve.

Mr. Morrow's hand engulfed Francis' as they shook.

As the lines shuffled and new men filed into the building, Young said, "I do have to admit, I grow more worried the longer the war drags."

Mr. Morrow watched Francis make his way to the uniform line. He could see Francis biting his lip, twisting his soft jawline.

"Worried about what, Young?"

"Have you seen a fit soldier this morning?"

"They aren't, I'll agree. But once they're in the field and under fire, I think they'll be some goddamn determined bastards to get back home, I'll tell you that."

Mr. Young turned to a fresh page in his ledger, dipped his pen into the inkwell and said, "We'll see."

Mr. Morrow spat the residue of his chew into the spittoon. Using his tongue, he repositioned the clump in his lip. He wiped his mouth with his hand, then wiped his hand on his thigh.

"Next!"

3

Inflating the Intrepid

Squinting through the late summer sun, soldiers could see the Capitol Dome partially constructed with scaffolding and cranes waiting beside it. They stood in rows in fields hemmed by the winding Potomac River, marching and drilling. The Washington Monument was being raised to the south. Unfinished, it stood like a landlocked lighthouse without a beacon. Still more soldiers moved in processions through the streets, spilling into the crops of tents raised in open space on the periphery of the city. The clear sky offered only uninterrupted sunlight that turned every standing man into a sundial.

Regiments from farther north were on their way to Virginia, reinvigorating the Union lines that the Rebels had frayed and breached. Wagons rolled into the encampment, weighed down with supplies. Sutlers and newspapermen weaved through the sea of men, toting their carts, vending relative luxuries of coffee and tobacco. Among the tents, rifles propped each other up in sets of three and small fire pits burned smokeless. The scent of coffee and gunpowder mingled in the air as men conversed and ate a late afternoon meal of hardtack.

New volunteers just in from Philadelphia bolstered the Pennsylvania 116th. They pitched their tents among the veterans, having been informed that they would have two days within view of the capital before moving farther south into Virginia.

One soldier set his tent near a cook fire with a kettle set in the glowing coals. Placing his back next to his raised

Inflating the Intrepid

tent, he stood surveying the scenery around him.

His face was hairless and plump. He did what he could to correct the wide-eyed, open-mouthed expression of a child at a carnival. Every person around him caught his attention, and he appeared both nervous and eager to meet everyone. A high, brittle voice came from the tent beside him.

"Would you like some coffee, there?"

An older gentleman emerged with thin hair slicked back into a ratty mane. His grin was missing teeth, creating a slight whistle that he fought to plug with his tongue as he spoke. "Seeing as how I just heated some up. Have a cup, boy."

The soldier politely declined and stood looking out beyond the fields of tents, out to where the Potomac was pinched in the distance by the thick growth of vegetation on the banks. The sun was on the descent, drawing long shadows off of both trees and men. Fife notes and the raps of a drummer boy at drill were carried on the wind into the camp, where men playing banjos and snares picked them up to pass the time.

A group of men broke into roaring laughter as a woman made her way through the tents. A smattering of applause spread to others who clapped without even knowing why.

The older soldier dismissed the boy with a single wave of his palm and crouched beside the fire pit with the steaming kettle.

"You looking for someone you know?" he asked, his back to the young man.

"No, sir."

The woman passed close to them now, her pale neck glowing. She grinned, seeming to bask in the gaze of so many eyes.

"Well, boy, you going to follow her home, or what?"

"Oh, no." He removed his hat and wrung it in his hands. "I just ain't seen this many people in all of my life."

The older man still crouched over the fire, facing away. "I thought you boys came down from Philadelphia. Lot of folks up there, I hear. Never been myself."

"Enlisting was my first time ever being there. But I can say, there was a near stampede getting on the train."

The old man stood and handed him a small tin cup of coffee. "Name's Harry."

"Samuel." He took the cup and raised it with an uncertain grin.

The old man echoed the gesture with a cup of his own. "So, Samuel, you aren't city folk, then?"

"No, sir. I'm more of a country boy."

Harry took a sip and spat the first mouthful onto the ground. "You sound like Ol' Billy Boy over here. Farmers, the two of you." He leaned on the front post of his tent with the crook of his elbow, shifted his weight onto one leg, and bent the other so that it balanced on the toe of his boot. From a distance, he might have appeared to be a scarecrow. "Well, Sam, you better get used to all these people. Your life'll very well depend on the lot of them."

Samuel nodded. "Safety in numbers and all the rest."

He held the coffee close to his nose and took a deep breath. He blew on the cup. His focus was now beyond the tents, in a far field where a small group was tending to what appeared to be a great tarp. The break in a tree line between the fields revealed two large, enclosed wagons with thick hoses flopping to the ground and disappearing behind the mules and soldiers. Men toting ropes flashed in and out of view.

"What do you suppose is going on over there?" Samuel asked.

"The—wait a minute. Dammit, what do you call it—aeronautics division," Harry said. "Going for a balloon ride, I guess."

"A balloon?"

"A hot air balloon. Boy, ain't you been around at all?"

INFLATING THE INTREPID

"Never seen one."

Samuel took a few careful pulls from his cup as the men crossed to the wagons and back, directed by a tall figure in black. A long line of cannons being pulled by horses cut his view. He poured the remainder out and placed the cup on a stone by the fire. "This is something I've got to see."

"Now hold on there, Sam, just hold on," Harry said. "I'll take a walk. Let me see about this other boy first." Harry drank from his cup, then cast the rest aside.

"Howe, get your ass out here," he said. "You ought to see some of the world while you're here, too. Herkommen, boy. Herkommen."

From another tent appeared a broad straw hat followed by the thin frame, lean with muscle, of the man underneath it. His beard grew in clusters and his large hands enveloped a notepad. He tipped the brim of his hat down to shade his eyes from the brilliant sun, and Samuel nodded in return.

He said only, "Where?"

"This here's Sam. He's new to the 116th. Wants to see this business about the balloon."

"Are the couriers in?"

"Yes, we can drop your damn letters. Known you a week and alls you're worried about are your goddamn letters. Stubborn goddamned Germans."

William reached for a tin cup beside the fire and shook it in Harry's direction.

"No more coffee?"

The open field radiated the sun's heat. Steam belched from the strange, enclosed wagons as air hissed through the serpentine hoses. The opening of the balloon yawned as the bulb inflated, the letters spelling *INTREPID* swelling on the side.

The boys in the camp beside the field struck up a rendition of "Yankee Doodle Dandy" and the raucous chorus

27

of the men singing drowned out the plucking banjos. Their song devolved into cheers as another woman promenaded by, her gown dragging along through the dirt. They applauded as a soldier caught up to her, wrapping her in an American flag. She curtsied to her admirers, soliciting more cheers.

"That man there is the professor," Harry said, pointing to a stern-faced man. "He runs the Balloon Corps." They watched as he circled the balloon and tended to the lines. Only his bottom lip would peek out from under his untrimmed and overgrown mustache as he barked commands to the men surrounding the balloon.

"Strange bird," Harry added.

Samuel was unable to conceal his fascination. "Seems so," he said.

"Tighter on that line," the man called. He leaned his weight against the rope in his hand. "It goes quick once it's started."

A soldier swung a hammer and hit high iron notes, driving a thick metal stake farther into the earth. With quick hands, he swung a thick rope around the peg and fastened a sailor's knot.

The rope creaked and the knot cinched as the balloon inflated, casting an enlarging shadow on the attending crew. The netting draped over the balloon drew tight. A line of muzzle blasts sounded in succession from the drills in the field beside them. The attending crew shouted and called back in alarm.

"They better mind the balloon," the professor called. "She's going to stand up. She'll stand."

Harry spread his arms and motioned for Sam and William to step back. Samuel stood dazed, his eyes widening as the balloon lurched into an upright position, spreading its shadow over him. The basket hovered a few feet off the ground, a dozen lines leading from the netting to the stakes. A smattering of claps came from the tents. The crown of the bulb stood proud above the tree line, and a

Inflating the Intrepid

number of soldiers stopped their drilling and camping to stand in admiration.

Samuel held his face rigid to hide his wonder at this new technology. He looked to William, who seemed altogether unimpressed.

William tilted his hat back to better see the spectacle of the floating giant, the men swarming about, the ropes and gas lines, the professor readying the rope ladder at the basket. He looked to the last of the horse-drawn cannons passing, then to the singing men, then to a man who had dismounted his horse wearing a satchel swollen with correspondence.

"It really is a marvel," Samuel said.

"Won't be so marvelous if they send a cannon ball through it. You ever seen a balloon like that, Ol' Bill?" Harry turned to see William marching off toward the postman with short, stiff strides. "Bill!"

Without turning around, William raised the pad in his hand and shook it.

"Him and his goddamn letters! Never seen a damn near illiterate boy slave so much over letters!"

The professor tending the balloon ran a spool of wire from the basket to a post near the spectating soldiers. His soaked collar was still buttoned up to the top. He wore his formal attire, as if he'd step from that very field into a classroom and begin a lecture on physical science.

"You there," he said to Samuel. "You hold this." He forced the spool into Samuel's chest.

"What is it?"

"We're rigging up a telegraph line to the *Intrepid*, there."

"This boy doesn't know the first thing about it," Harry said.

"Not many do," the professor replied. "We'd be the first to do it."

Samuel looked down at the spool of wire, concealing a grin.

The professor continued, "It's only for a moment. I have letters to send." He produced envelopes from the inner lining of his coat. He flashed them to Harry and said, "Direct to Lincoln."

Splitting Harry and Samuel, he headed off to where William was in conversation with the courier. The balloon bobbed against the currents of a strong breeze, lurching against the anchor points. The men tending the lines called to one another, moving from the wagons to ropes and back again.

Harry inspected the wire. "Heavy," he said. "Wonder why they're sending it up in the balloon."

"To signal down," Samuel said. "They'll get high enough for a good view and tap down what they see."

"Now how could that possibly work with this simple wire?" Harry inspected the loose end of the spool. "Nothing more than chicken wire without the barb."

"Beats drawing it." Samuel unspooled a small length of the wire. "They say pretty soon there will be telegraph wire along every road for communication."

"Well, boy, I'll tell you what. In times of war, I'd rather look at a drawing than whatever they're supposing that this'll produce."

"I'm going to ask that professor if I might be able to get in the balloon with him."

Harry took the spool of wire from him. "Boy," he said, "this isn't a pony ride."

Samuel took in the scale of the balloon, ignoring Harry. It now rose some fifty feet in the air and cast an eclipsing shadow over the onlookers. The crew in the field loosened a few of the lines, and it climbed even higher. Even they seemed impressed as they tilted back their caps to gaze up at the levitating giant.

The professor returned from the courier and issued a sharp, shrieking whistle. He held out his arms and swept them down, calling, "Down! Bring her down, goddammit!"

A few men called to each other, two mules began to

tow lines attached to pulleys, and the balloon descended.

Harry remained focused on Samuel. "Just you ask him, then. I can't wait to see how he responds. 'To hell with you,' he'll say."

The professor was shaking hands with the courier, who made to mount his horse. The sun was setting, and some cloud cover was threatening from the north. Shadows were merging and swelling now, the sun quarter set. William had disappeared from view.

The balloon loomed large in the setting sun. A small crowd formed at the edge of the encampment admiring the scene.

The professor approached for the wire with a letter in his hand. His mustache was so untamed that it slightly muffled his speech. In conversation, the subtle movements of his lips were completely hidden.

"The wire, there?" he asked. His demeanor had changed. He took the spool and unwound a length of telegraph wire only to wind it back on tighter, all the while shaking his head and thinking.

Samuel spoke. "Professor, sir. I was wondering if you might need assistance in the balloon—when it lifts."

"I may," the professor said. "Whenever we do get her into the air."

"Sorry, sir?"

"Won't be tonight, lad. You're on the move. Just got word." He tucked the spool under his armpit and removed a letter from an inner coat pocket. He read it again, shook his head, and tucked it away before walking off toward the balloon hanging low and half lit in the field.

Harry had left, too. Off to break down his campsite and prepare for marching. Buglers echoed each other's calls from one end of the camp to the other, stirring every man into action.

The regiments from the fields trickled into the camp, where the white tents flashed and disappeared like lightening bugs at dusk. The balloon folded and sulked back to the earth as the professor hollered commands to his crew.

The raps of a snare drum popped along the road.

Samuel made his way back to his tent, but he had trouble locating it with the previous rows having evaporated. He located Harry by his scarecrow silhouette, arms reaching wide to fold his canvas tent. The embers of his cook fire glowed deep red along the dark ground beside him.

"Any word on where we're heading?"

"Boy, you better stop looking around and get packed."

Harry's face had lost whatever geniality it could muster. In the low light, the wrinkles on his face were deep gouges, and the blue roots of his beard darkened his features. Crouching over his fire pit, his face glowed, and his intermittent teeth flashed like embers. "I'll leave you a cup of coffee here, but I ain't waiting for you."

Samuel's face dropped, and he began breaking down his tent. He offered no response to Harry as he removed the tent posts from the canvas.

Harry offered an apology by means of explanation. "The older you are, the closer you want to be to the front of the march. That way, you can fall behind without being left behind."

"Makes sense, old timer," Samuel said. "Thanks for the coffee. I'll be sure to return the cup."

"That's the point." Harry heaped his pack on and marched off toward where buglers were rallying and organizing groups of men.

Samuel hurried to ready his pack. The majority of the encampment had been taken up.

A dark figure approached, with a broad brim that Samuel recognized as William even in silhouette. "The 116th is gathering by that tree line over there." He used the barrel of his rifle to point.

"Thanks. Did you get to send your letters?"

William crouched and retrieved a tin cup from the fire. "The courier is going south. I need someone headed north." He tipped the cup to Samuel and walked off to the cluster of trees.

Samuel lifted his pack, crouched for his cup of coffee, and looked out over the empty field where the encampment had been a thriving city only an hour ago.

The capital building and the Washington Monument caught the last few rays of sunlight on their white stone facades. Through the dark smoke of the doused fires and the trampled state of the landscape, it took on the appearance of a fallen civilization.

Night lowered fast on the Potomac as the soldiers of the Union Army made their way into Virginia.

4

SOLDIERS & PATIENTS

Day broke over the hollowed-out town of Fredericksburg. Old snow and mud were frosted along the roads, with a sharp wind whipping off of the Rappahannock. Pillars of smoke billowed from the forested campsites of townsfolk who had been forced to trade positions with the rising tide of soldiers. They had abandoned their town only for troops to occupy and then raid it for anything to fend off the cold other than their meager rations of hardtack and army issued blankets.

The sunrise cut through the haze, illuminating the top of Marye's Heights to the west. Glinting Confederate bayonets flashed like sparks atop the ridge, and as the sun rose, the light washed down the hill and into the city, where the men in Union Blue were huddled in the shadows of the abandoned town. The river divided the town, and on its shores broken ice sheets piled one upon the other like unfinished tombstones.

A man strode away from the eastern shore. Carrying a medical field kit, he made his way up a small hill to a barn.

The day lightened and the Union soldiers trickled through the town's streets, gathering into formations. Officers in the back wagged their fingers, nodded, debated, and circled their horses around one another. The men at the edge of the city congregated in quiet groups, equipping themselves and watching the sun rise without any offering of heat. A frozen misty haze hung in the air.

On top of the little knoll, about a half a mile away,

Soldiers and Patients

the man stood waiting. Looking over the thin frame of his glasses, his face downturned and his eyes pushing up against a furrowed brow, he watched the soldiers amassing. Men in lay clothing circled a small cluster of white tents at the edge of the town. With a full wheelbarrow, they were still clearing out the dismembered limbs and soiled linens from the early contact the day before.

He waited at a fork in the road. Squinting, he could see a slender white figure materialize from a wooded patch. As his breath rose in clouds around his balding head, the ghost bobbed its way along the icy road toward him.

"Good morning, Claire. I've got to admit, I'm surprised to see you," he said.

Her pale form had a red face, reddest at the tip of her nose. She wore a sun blanket over her shoulders and a homespun scarf over her head to warm the ears.

"I didn't think I was even coming, to be honest with you, Doctor," she said.

The doctor nodded in the direction of the barn and together they made their way.

He yawned and wiped his face, "How are they making out in the woods? Awful time to be without a home."

"My mother nearly froze last night. She'd rather that I stay with the family today and help gather up some supplies." She paused as if she were still considering the idea. "My father thinks it's right courageous of me, though. 'Those boys are all American,' he said. Gave me the key to the house to get in the cellar. Said there's a jug of whiskey in there you can use."

"We'll need most of the linens, too."

"Word got back to them that the boys have been helping themselves in a lot of the homes along the main streets. The whole town is ransacked. They're worried it's in ruins before the real fighting even starts."

"Them boys are trying to survive, just like them in the woods. Both parties just needed to find a way to make it until this morning." The doctor let a shiver run its course through him. "Feels like all hell's about to break loose on those boys. I think after today it will be over."

All at once, mustering music and morale, the Union soldiers began to hum and cluster together. Bugles sounded as they ran hollering from the shadows of the town onto the sunlit hill. Responding in kind, the Rebels at the top rested their barrels on a stone wall and began laying men to rest at the midpoint of the hill. The air shook with a cacophonous earth-born thunder and lightning, a boiling sea of smoke, muzzle flashes, and rumbling artillery. Blue union coats fell in clusters, swallowed up by an avalanche of smoke.

Claire stood in awe. She was nearly forced to shout. "I've never seen so many people in all my life."

The doctor pressed his glasses flush onto his face with a trembling index finger.

"Let's hurry. Joseph is already at the barn."

In the barn, thin shards of light spilled through gaps in the wood and the perforations of bullet holes from the day before. The beams of light spread wider from their points of entry, severed by the sporadic flight of flies. The hayloft overflowed, spilling the crop below as a welcome insulation for the barn. A stable door had been laid across sawhorses. Beside it was a small hay cart, which a young native boy unloaded with a pitchfork.

"Joseph, we'll need more water," the doctor said. "More water, and quite a few more branches for crutches."

Without a word, the boy jogged out with an empty pail and went off crunching through the frosted field to the well.

"Won't be long now," the doctor said. He placed his medical kit on the makeshift table and tilted the lid up.

The earth trembled from a barrage of heavy artillery. Man-made thunder that rattled some of the shovels and rakes from their perch on the wall. The calls of the men in

Soldiers and Patients

the field broke through the sporadic pops and hisses of the musket fire.

Joseph came clanking through the doorway, hugging a bundle of crutch-length branches. "There is a trough half full of water outside. Worried it'll freeze," he said.

The doctor went to speak but paused to let a series of cannon blasts run their course. When he could speak, he said, "Run with Claire to the house. Grab all the linens you can find. She said there's whiskey."

Claire made eye contact with Joseph to make sure he heard the doctor over the cacophony. "God almighty it's loud," she said as the two exited the large doorway, ducking from invisible debris.

The doctor moved to the open doorway and hollered after them, "The first wagon will be here soon!" His voice fell mute against the racket in the field. Successive musket blasts flashed from the stone wall at the top of the hill. The blue waves of Union soldiers lapped against the hillside and reseeded. Musket smoke rolled in like a fog from the hilltop down to the river. The doctor looked down along the snaking dirt road and saw a horse-drawn wagon making its way to the barn.

Men tailed behind the wagon, limping along and gripping upper body injuries. The soldier driving the wagon rounded the horse under a large spruce tree beside the barn, scattering a handful of crows from the branches above. The less-injured helped the more severely wounded to the ground. Some bodies remained after the living had dismounted. With a nod to the doctor, the soldier flicked the reins and headed back toward the chaotic haze of the battlefield with the horse at a canter.

Claire and Joseph returned from the house. About a dozen men positioned themselves on the bare soil beneath the spruce, moaning, panting, and writhing. Joseph administered water.

"Gentlemen," the doctor said. "I practice medicine about twenty miles from here." His head was pitched down so he could gaze over his bifocals and assess the men. "You came to me because the field hospital yonder is already overwhelmed. I'm one man. I'll do my best." He pressed his frames flush to his face and pointed a long finger at a soldier reclined against the tree. "Is this young man gut shot?"

"He is," a comrade said.

"I need some of you who are able to help him into the barn."

Two crows perched on a fence post, provoked into curiosity by the activity. Joseph scattered them with a rock.

"Joseph," the doctor said. "More water."

The doctor was quick into the barn, retrieving a long pair of tongs from the medical kit.

"Claire, a rag with some chloroform."

The first soldier was laid on the table, and the men who positioned him stepped off to the side as the doctor approached. One was an older Irishman with a shoulder wound. The other had a light colored, unkempt beard that grew in patches. He had no visible injury but was pale and shaking from loss of blood. The gut-shot soldier rocked his head from side to side on the table, appearing to make an effort to stay in the present moment. His arms were held stiff with his hands overlapping on his abdomen.

"You're safe now, friend. Your name?"

"O'Connor," he said as if waking from a dream. "O'Connor. Pennsylvania 116th."

"All right, O'Connor. Claire here is going to press some chloroform over your face. Help dull the pain a bit. Nothing to fear."

Claire approached from above the soldier's head and applied the rag. At first the soldier stirred, but he relaxed back into a subtle rocking motion. The doctor was able to raise the boy's arms with hardly even a response.

After peeling away the tattered shirt and rinsing the

wound with water, a fairly clean hole was revealed on the side of the soldier's abdomen. With each exhale, black blood bubbled from the gaping wound. As the doctor inserted his instrument, the soldier startled into wakefulness.

He wailed and reached for the doctor as the other soldiers pinned him back down. "God almighty!" he screamed, baring his teeth in pain.

The doctor hunched over the wound, probing. The tongs met the tip of the round and only pushed it farther into the soldier.

Raising only his eyes, the doctor consulted his patient.

"O'Connor, you've lost a lot of blood. That bullet is buried deep. Nearly to your back. I could wound you worse trying to retrieve it. Your only chance is to suffer through it."

The soldier receded into himself, fighting for composure. He focused his energy and spoke through gasps. "A Priest? Last rights?"

"Joseph, there's a Bible on the workbench."

The boy was quick to the workbench and back.

The soldier flailed on the table; his companions unable to hold him. "A priest," he gritted through his teeth, "a priest!"

"I have the text here. It's best to be calm."

"Not a redskin." He coughed and squeezed his abdomen, panting. "A priest."

The boy backed away from the table in fear of the dying soldier. He crouched where the mountains of hay spilled from above. The boy's eyes were on the doctor while the doctor's remained on his patient.

"What passage would you like to hear?" the doctor insisted.

O'Connor wept and writhed in silence for a moment. His knees curled up and then kicked out, knocking his heels against the table.

"Leave me be, witch doctor."

"I have it here. Just tell me the passage."

The soldier rolled onto his side and lurched his body off of the table. He doubled over in pain but regained his balance. Dragging his feet for a few final steps, he shuffled to a corner of the barn and reclined against a bale of hay where he began reciting the *Our Father*.

"Joseph, rinse the table. He'll do you no harm. Claire, that man may have some of your father's whiskey."

Emerging from the barn, the doctor braced against the wall of sound. The din of the battle was at a high point. The hillside was stained a muddy red, and bodies lay about as though they'd fallen from the sky. The doctor's hands felt biting cold, being wet in the open December air. He wiped them in rough swipes to both clean and warm them. His were bloody about the shirt cuffs and waist, in the manner of a butcher.

"You," the doctor amplified his voice against the concussive explosions. "Your leg is hit bad? Boys, boys! Bring him in next!"

※

A new soldier rested on the table, hit high in the thigh bone by a musket ball. Claire readied fresh linens. Joseph stood back to avoid attention, his eyes focused, his face hard as wood, still clutching the Bible against his chest.

"Peter," the soldier offered through chattering teeth. "Name's Peter." He attempted to sit up and inspect the leg himself. "It's splintered badly. I can't do hardly anything to stop the bleeding." He composed himself. "I took a shirt from a body in the field, doctor. I did. I stuffed it clear into the hole to stop the bleeding. But I couldn't stop it. It wouldn't stop."

"Claire, the syringe from my kit, please." The doctor cocked his head down and spoke softly as he inspected the wound. "Splintered. It is splintered."

The doctor raised his head and looked to the back wall of the barn. The midday sun hung in ribbons along the

Soldiers and Patients

assortment of tools as they shook on their perches from the pounding munitions; several shovels, soil rakes, a scythe, and a sturdy buck saw with a fresh blade.

Prone on the table, Peter watched the doctor with wide eyes. He took notice of O'Connor, lying in a thatch of hay with one arm beneath his head, the other resting gently over his side. He looked as though he were asleep and dreaming.

A lull settled in the fighting and men's voices could be heard reorganizing their efforts. The gray sky thinned, and the sunlight brightened. The shuffling movements of Joseph and Claire had scattered hay about the floor which now clung to the bloody soles of their shoes. A crow fluttered in the open hayloft, twitched and cawed, and flew away. The beams of light sharpened in the cloud movement, drawing the spilled blood into a bright red hue. The doctor knelt beside O'Connor, checking his pulse.

"Is he going to wake up, Doctor?"

The doctor hung his head for a moment. The rip of musket fire sounded from the field, answered from Marye's Heights by a rolling thunder of booming cannons. The barn shook and the light thinned. Lifting his head, the doctor reached for the buck saw.

"Joseph," he said. "Soon you'll need to take these shovels. You'll take them outside and tell any of the able bodied to start digging a ditch. Tell them to come get O'Connor. Put the Bible back on the work bench."

Peter trembled as the doctor approached. A horse and wagon rattled past the open door. The shouting of men was close, but unintelligible.

Claire said, "You'll feel just a pinch. Like a bee sting." She administered the syringe along his hip. The doctor watched the syringe with red-rimmed eyes, flexing his grip on the handles of the saw.

"Now the chloroform rag. Joseph, the rope please. This will be a very high cut."

Wielding the buck saw, the doctor waved to the

wounded Irishman and his sickly companion. They approached and braced Peter's shoulders. Joseph looped a heavy rope around the table and cinched a knot to the soldier's midsection. His head bobbed back and forth as his body relaxed.

"Ten minutes, boys," the doctor called. "Ten minutes." And then, to himself, "This'll be a high cut."

For a moment he stared down at the exposed leg, considering the relation of the wound to the hip. Using the full length of the blade, the doctor began to take long, sweeping strokes with the saw. The body flinched only at the contact; the saw began to shudder as they raked through the bone.

Claire circulated linens around them, giving the doctor a clear line of sight and keeping the table from being soaked. Her clothes were now stained through and warm against her skin.

Peter's arms and unlimbered leg began to wobble and flail. He started banging his head against the table with increasing force. The doctor released the saw, attempting to keep his waist flush against the table. A guttural scream rose above the racket of the battle.

"More chloroform, Claire!"

With her shaking hands, Claire doused the rag with a heavy dose. She smothered his face with the rag as Peter wrenched against it. Again, the soldier fell still. His body released a great exhale.

The cannon fire had ceased for the moment—only the static clicks of organized musket blasts could be heard. The doctor finished his work, pointing for the bandaged body to be placed near the bales of hay. The body was limp as they carried it to where O'Connor's had rested.

By dusk the tracks that surrounded the barn had been stomped to a bloody mud. Soldiers loitered around the front and the back of the building in various stages of agony and repair. Claire and John had organized a line of the more minor wounds, which they cleaned and bandaged, one after the other, while the doctor slept in a nearby canvas tent.

As he awoke, the darkening sky evoked an adrenaline rush that hurried him out of the tent and back toward the makeshift medical outpost. A bitterly cold wind was coming on with nightfall. He approached a trough of icy water to wash his face and hands.

Leaning against the wall of the barn, as if waiting for him, was a soldier with no apparent injury. He hid his face beneath the brim of a farmer's straw hat, ladling water into a canteen.

The doctor looked out into the field where the fighting had long subsided. Bodies crowded like flocks of black sheep in the fields. Turkey vultures had begun circling and perching in the windbreaks.

The doctor methodically removed his glasses and hooked them on his collar and leaned over the trough looking into his fluid reflection. The soldier beside him corked his canteen and asked, "Are you the doctor here?"

"I am." With quick scoops he rinsed his face.

"I need your attention just for a moment." As the doctor returned his glasses to his face, he could see a shiver run through the soldier's body. He was gaunt, wide eyed, and carried only a satchel and a canteen. Looking closer, the doctor could see that the man was wearing two layers of coats to withstand the oncoming cold.

"Are you gut shot?"

"No." His patchy beard looked rusted with dirt. He winced with pain as he spoke. "But I often feel like I was." He was eager to have gained the doctor's attention. "I've been fighting this dysentery for weeks. My gut is rotted out."

A short series of musket fire broke out along the base of the hill as Union soldiers attempted to recover injured soldiers from the fold. The vultures picked up from the trees and climbed in elevation moving away from the fighting.

"I've been in this camp for over a week. Spent all last night and this morning down on that hill."

Another soldier overheard. "Shoot the bastard! Don't waste the doctor's time."

"Now listen. Listen." The doctor turned to those congregated outside of the barn. "I will treat open wounds only. If you are deathly ill, like this one here, join with the others around back and lend a hand digging the ditch. When you're quite sick and tired of digging, lie in the damned hole!"

A heavy artillery bombardment shook the earth like a pulse.

All eyes were drawn back to the battlefield. At the base of the hill teams of men were struggling through muddy ruts with carts and wagons of dead and injured. The whole world seemed to be smoldering, churning smoke and bloody residue. Cloud cover had reduced the sun to a glowing orb floating just above the horizon.

"Where am I to go? How many of us are going to die in our sleep?"

The doctor watched a body being dragged from the barn, digging a single rut as they carried the dead weight to the pile out back. Most of the dead were now undressed, as survivors prepared for nightfall by scavenging extra layers from the fallen.

"Look around," he said. "You look the part of a farmer. What do you have in your barn to treat gut rot?"

"I haven't been educated like you, though. What can I do?"

"Are you German?"

The soldier studied the doctor. "I am"

"Drink and pray." Pointing at a soldier nursing a hand wound, the doctor said, "That hand hit by a musketball?"

The soldier could only nod to the doctor's advance.

"All right, get the hell inside. Likely you'll lose that

hand. Joseph, Claire, I'm starting this up again!"

With a tightened grip on the bucksaw, the doctor returned to the barn.

5

Photographing the Dead

A stripped-out tree line that edged the trampled corn field severed the rising sun into slices. The bodies of fallen soldiers filled the field like a crop, swollen and rotting like old pumpkins. Vultures congregated in a wake, perched on crooked limbs with black wings spread wide, warming.

A single rider made his way along the field, drawing an enclosed wagon behind his chestnut-colored horse. He craned his neck to survey the landscape. The horse slowed to a trot and stopped where the last few posts of a fence remained. Dismounting, the rider detached the horse from the wagon and tied it off on the fence.

He crouched and gathered a handful of gravel from the trail, which he spilled into the pocket of his dark wool coat. The sunlight fell in fingers across the field; the steam rising in light and dark ribbons. He scooped another handful.

His wind-burned cheeks were pink, reddening to the tip of his pointed nose. He wore a short-brimmed beaver twill hat, as black as his coat, gloves, and boots. Light snow and ice and the rotting soldiers made the whole world gray.

Picking his way through the field, the man scattered the vultures with stones from his pocket. "Get! Get the hell gone!" he called. When they had scattered, he walked in among the bodies.

He searched along, nudging to see if they were frozen through and locked into the earth. The soil had been trampled under the panicked tracks of soldiers in battle, and in the aftermath, it appeared tilled and ready for planting.

Many of the bodies were half nude, their uniforms having been salvaged by the living. Their pale skin looked like mottled clumps of old snow.

A group of a dozen soldiers had formed a circle, with a large, discharged shell in the center. Upon further inspection, the shell had been used as a make-shift fire pit. The men in the circle had not been killed in that formation but had crawled to it in the night. They were reclined in various poses, primitive dressings on mortal wounds. They appeared to have passed peacefully, falling asleep in the company of one another.

"Trying to keep warm? A little company for you?" The rider stood silhouetted in the center of the field like a scarecrow. He looked to his horse as it snorted and gave its harness a shake. The wagon tilted in the brunt of a strong gust of wind.

"I can be a little company for you boys," he said, a shiver in his voice. "A bit too late, I'm afraid."

He glanced around before dragging a fallen fence rail to the fire ring. He took his place.

"Better late than never, I suppose."

Reaching into an inner pocket of his coat, he produced a pipe, which he packed with tobacco. Patting his chest, he said, "My damned matches."

A soldier was lying on his back beside him, half sunken in the mud. His blue coat was frozen crisp. The rider took a deep breath and held it, then pinched the blue flap with the tips of his fingers and folded it open. He poked at the contents of the inner pockets. Finding no matches, he exhaled and moved to the next soldier in the ring.

Crouching beside him, the man looked closely at the soldier's pale face. "Looks like you're only napping, friend. Any matches on your person?"

The soldier was resting against the body of another, with his hands folded about his stomach. The rider lifted the soldier's hand and recoiled at how flaccid the corpse was. He let the arm drop and stood to survey the field.

His horse picked at the browned grasses reaching from the bottom of the fencepost. The vultures hopped from body to body at the far end of the field.

Returning his focus to the soldier, he said, "Some hole in your belly there. Still bleeding even after that young heart of yours has stopped." The soldier's breast pocket yielded a set of damp matches. "Thank you, friend. I will return the favor in what way I can."

Returning to his seat, the rider struck the matches and lit the pipe. After a few tugs, he whispered, "Such a toll. Such a toll."

The sun was now beginning to crest the tree line, spilling uncontested light into the field. It was clear where each army's soldiers had originated from. The bodies in the field wore the deep blue coats, now scattered about like black sheep crowding the pasture. The Confederates could be seen closer to the wooded lot, their yellow and gray uniforms piled like a stacked stone wall along the edge of the field. The forest behind the wall had been their protection.

The rider rested his head on his hand, prodding the ashes in the fire pit with the ram rod of a musket.

"I aim to show the North what you boys have been through. I really do."

At the far end of the field, two vultures bickered over a soldier's remains. One tugged at the open flesh of the neck, while the other hopped from the ground up to the soldier's bent and frozen leg.

"How long you boys think the devil will stay in this field?"

A third vulture joined the fray. They tugged at the open flesh of his face, clucking as they gulped rags of skin from the corpse.

The rider drew on his pipe. Exhaling, he said, "Devil don't know his riches here."

He reached for a soldier's rifle and searched the satchel at his side. He found two cartridges and began loading the musket. He placed the primer and cocked the rifle. Leaning his elbow on his knee, the rider fired at the vultures. They labored into the air, flying only a short distance before they perched and began casting blame at one another. He reloaded the rifle, cocked, and fired again.

The rider jumped as a voice called out, "Get out of there, grave robber!"

He turned to his horse, which now stood on six legs. A figure looked out from over the saddle.

The rider bit his pipe and spoke from the side of his mouth. "Who is it there?"

"A soldier of the Union Army. You leave these men."

The rider removed the pipe from his mouth. His voice trembled as he spoke. "Are you a ghost then?"

"Not yet."

The rider stood, holding the rifle at his side. "I'm not robbing these bodies."

The man's blue cap bobbed behind the saddle as the horse sneezed and shook its bridle chains.

"I said I ain't robbing these boys."

"I heard."

"Well, move along then. I'm tending to something."

"Leave this field and I'll let you be."

"I said I have business here."

"I say you do not."

The rider took a drag from his pipe as he looked down at the fire pit. "Show me you are unarmed." He cleared his throat. "I can explain myself rightly, but I'm not approaching until I know you'll not harm me."

The soldier stepped out from behind the horse. Tall and thin, he wore his Union uniform and carried nothing but a satchel over his shoulder.

The solider fought a heavy cough, cleared his throat, and spat. "Let's have it, then," he said, wiping his mouth on his sleeve.

The rider propped the gun against its owner and took high steps back through the field. The warm sun was on his back, and the odor of decay rose in faint clouds from the bodies.

Taking in the soldier up close, he seemed gaunt and malnourished.

"I'm a photographer," the rider said. "I've come to photograph some of these battlegrounds to the North."

"Not much to show them. Awful waste."

"Well, that's exactly what I aim to show. It's gone on long enough, wouldn't you say?"

"I would."

"Well, what's your story?"

"Haven't got one."

"You fought with these men?"

"Men like them."

The photographer packed more tobacco into his pipe. He looked at the soldier's pale skin, and the knuckles of his thin wrists that hung out of his tattered sleeves.

"You're sure you're not a ghost? Never seen someone so pale in all my life."

The soldier only looked out over the field, scratching at the patch of hair on his jaw.

"Are you here to bury the men, then?" the photographer said. "You haven't got a shovel."

"I am on my way home."

"Where to?"

"My home."

The photographer offered the soldier some of his tobacco and, upon refusal, carefully closed the tin and placed it in a saddle bag on his horse.

"Well, sir. I do say good luck on your journey. Sounds like quite the walk."

"Well, be on your way, then." The soldier's fingers wrapped around the photographer's arm like the talons of a buzzard. He was frail, yet his grip was rigid.

"No, sir. Let go."

"I'm not leaving you to bother the dead. Let these men rest."

"You've got it wrong, friend." He wrenched his arm free. "I'm going to photograph these men to show that all is not gallant in the field of war. Wouldn't you like the public to know?"

"They can't know a thing like war."

"Oh, but they will," a grin sprouted on the photographer's face, "and if you help me, it'll all go quicker."

"I've no desire to help."

"Well, sir. Care to make a deal?"

The soldier coughed again and spat. He offered no other response. Seeing an opportunity to bargain, the photographer outlined the job at hand, ending, "And for your help, I'll ride you one hundred miles in any direction you so choose. Towards home, I'd suppose. North?"

The soldier looked from the field to the photographer, and back to the field.

"Wagon's pretty warm. Old Agnes here is a smooth stride." He patted the hindquarter of the horse.

The soldier offered his hand. "William."

The photographer patted the top of his hand as they shook. "J. R. Johnstone. Friend, we'll be quick about this business and then make up for your lost time tenfold."

Johnstone clapped his hand on William's shoulder and began to outline the scope of their labor.

"A boy in the field over there, near that smoke plume there, he's still soft enough to pose. We might be able to position him in good light. It sounds awful, I know, but we could make quite an impression with a well-framed shot. Give him the chance to change the war before he rots afield."

William rubbed the back of his neck as he rounded to the back of the wagon. He crouched for a stone, which he launched at the vultures. Turning to Johnstone, he took a deep breath, approached the wagon, and swung the door open.

Johnstone stood at the fire pit, eyeing his subject. William made his second trip back to the wagon for another crate of photography equipment.

Speaking to himself, Johnstone said, "Right. Well. I apologize in advance, young man."

He steadied his shaking hands and eased the soldier into an upright sitting position, propped up by a rail of the fence. A breath of air escaped the body as the stomach contracted. Retrieving the rifle, he propped it on the rail beside the soldier. He took a step back to see the pose in whole. Leaning back in, he rested the musket across the soldier's thigh. Johnstone pinched the cuff of the sleeve to move the boy's hand from the wound in his abdomen to the stock of the rifle when a faint whisper slipped out of the soldier.

Stepping back, Johnstone called to William. "He's alive! Christ, he's alive!"

"Can't be!"

"He spoke. He did. I heard it! He spoke!"

William made his way through the bodies, removing a canteen from his satchel.

Johnstone crouched beside the soldier and held his ear close to his face.

"Did I just hear his last? Oh, Lord. He may have just said his last. I couldn't hear. . ."

Pushing Johnstone back, William tilted the soldier's head and poured water into his mouth. The soldier's eyes fought to roll open. They were bloodshot and yellowed, flickering open and closed again.

"Lay him down flat," William said. "Prop his head, there. Make him comfortable."

Again, the voice rose from the soldier.

"Pictures!" Johnstone said. "He's saying 'pictures'. God, does he know what I'm doing?" Johnstone threw both of his hands to the top of his hat. "I'll be cursed my whole life—"

"No. *His* pictures, likely. He must want to see his darling."

William opened the boy's coat and vest. A pocket sewn into his shirt held a photo case. Removing and opening it, William nodded. "He has a wife and a daughter here." He handed it to Johnstone.

With shaking hands, the photographer looked upon the soldier's loved ones. "Lovely shot," he said. Trembling, he held it open in front of the soldier's face. "See? See here, young man?"

The soldier's eyes cracked open, welled with tears, and pinched shut. His face contorted into a sorrowful expression with sagging cheeks. A coughing sob took his body. He rolled onto his side, gasping for his last few cold breaths. He spat mouthfuls of blood as he exhaled. His body fell into a quiet shiver, and then became still. William held his hand on the soldier's shoulder, his head down. The vultures cackled in the distance, one lifting into the air and flying off.

Johnstone's mouth flexed and widened.

William stared out toward the vultures. The sun was ascending behind the birds, and their shadows stretched toward the men.

"Let me take your horse," William said.

Wiping his face, Johnstone said, "The hell are you talking about?"

"I need to get to my family. Let me take your horse."

"Are you mad? I can make meaning of this man's death. Don't you see?" From inside his coat pocket, he retrieved a handkerchief, folded it, and patted it against his nose and mouth. "People need to see this."

He watched as William reached into his satchel.

"Don't you draw on me. . ."

Johnstone flinched as William produced a bundle of letters.

"Letters?"

"Will you take these to the nearest post office when you're done?"

"Well, now. Hold on."

"Please. They'll send word to my wife."

"What's stopping you from sending them?"

"I can't wander into town. They'll arrest me."

"What I'm doing here isn't necessarily legal, friend."

"I'm a deserter. I'll be hanged."

Johnstone refocused on the fetal position of the soldier's body.

"This man just died." Johnstone rubbed his palms against his eyes and lifted his hat to scratch at his hair. "This man just died."

Johnstone stood up and marched toward his horse. William placed his letters back into his bag, closed the photo case and tucked it under the soldier's arm, then followed the photographer to his horse.

"I will send them under one circumstance." Johnstone unloaded the tripod from the wagon.

The soldier sharpened his gaze and focused his attentions on Johnstone's eyes.

"I will deliver your letters if you let me take your portrait."

William shook his head. "Not a good idea."

"No one will see this photo for weeks. And far from here. It will remain anonymous. You may be a sickly sight to behold, but your face will tell quite a story."

"Please. I've helped you some. Just take this postage."

The thunder of hooves sounded, flushing the vultures out of the field. The Union flag came first into view, waving over one of the riders. Johnstone watched as a team of horsemen rounded the shoulder of the field, from the same direction that he had come.

"Looks like your friends are looking for you," Johnstone said. He turned to see that William had ducked behind the stone wall bordering the road.

Johnstone set the legs of his tripod and motioned to shut the door of the wagon. Pressed between the door and the frame were the bundle of letters, which he tucked into the inner paneling.

PHOTOGRAPHING THE DEAD

The lead cavalryman was a big man with a booming voice. His chin tucked itself into his bulbous neck as he looked down from his horse at Johnstone. "What business do you have here?"

"I'm a photographer, sir."

"That much is obvious. Name?"

"J. R. Johnstone."

"Whereabouts are you from?"

"Just south of New York City. Come a long way to document—"

"Name's Hanover. These men here are going to be burying your subjects. Now, I've no issue with you taking some photographs, so long as you stay—"

"Sir?"

Hanover scanned the field, turning his horse in slow steps. To his men he said, "You hear coughing?"

One soldier dismounted and inspected Johnstone's wagon. "Appears to be alone."

A long-limbed horseman in back said, "Could've been one of them in the field."

"Can't be survivors," Hanover said. "Bloodiest goddamn skirmish and cold as hell last night."

"Never know," the horseman said. He watched a vulture fly over them, displaying his knotted Adam's apple. "Can't know a thing like that," he said.

"You could dig over there," Johnstone said. "Softer soil."

"Says who?" Hanover lifted his head and peered hard down at Johnstone. "Why would it matter?"

"No, well, the soil there, sir, it isn't frozen." Johnstone picked up his tripod and took a quiet breath. "Boys had a fire, soil never iced over."

Hanover's brow contorted. He trotted his horse around Johnstone's wagon, then out into the field where the wisp of smoke rose in threads. "Seems so," he called. "Good bit of bodies here, as well. Well, boys, let's have at it."

The soldiers all dismounted and unstrapped their shovels from their horses. They made their way toward Hanover as he walked his horse through the field, pressing against the bodies to see how thawed they'd become. Johnstone carried his tripod toward the fire pit. The wind picked up, and he turned his back to lean into it. A dark figure flashed and then disappeared in the wood line to the north.

6

FRIENDS AND ENEMIES

"Yankees!" he called from the far bank. "Yankees! Show yourselves!"

A man stood in tattered butternut pants along the shore, his sleeves rolled, skipping stones into the water. His sun-faded jacket hung heavy over branches where his rifle leaned. He shouted across the river.

"You've nothing to fear, ya cowards! Let's see ya, boys."

It was late winter and the small disturbance on the water caused ripples that cracked the thin ring of ice where water met land. The sun was warm and the thawed soil beneath his feet softened as he shifted his weight. He watched the steep opposing bank where he could see a well-worn path down to the water. In the distance a large Union camp had been turning farm fields into frozen mud for the better part of three weeks.

From the brush along a rise in the bank emerged a Union soldier, rifle in hand. "What business have you here?" he called. "Scout?"

"Scout? What scout comes this close in plain view? Calls out to the other?" The Rebel soldier drew his accent out with a slow cadence. "How long have you been a soldier, boy?"

"Quite long enough, you inbred. Get away from here."

He nuzzled the stock of his rifle into his shoulder and tightened his grip. "You wouldn't be the first Reb I shot."

"Well, this would be a right and fancy execution. Seeing as how we're not here to fight."

Notes from a Deserter

The Union soldier now counted ten Rebel soldiers in all sitting on the bank, in varying reclined poses, all unarmed.

The Rebel offered a casual salute and tossed a stone into the stream. The Yankee flinched and raised his barrel.

"You've nothing to fear, Yank. One of us would've shot you when we saw you sulking in that brush. If we wished you dead, that is."

The Union soldier loosened the grip of his rifle and looked back the way he came, giving a silent nod. Four of his comrades emerged from the overgrowth on the bankside. As the soldiers stepped into the open, little rocks tumbled down into the stream.

"Give 'em hell, Butch," they said.

"Well, what brings you here, you sons of bitches?" Butch relaxed his shooting form and held the gun loose and horizontal at his side. He turned his head slightly downstream to better hear a response.

"Hold down that mean spirit." The Rebel soldier tilted his hat back and flared his eyes. "We mean to trade, not holler and cuss at one another."

"We got orders not to fraternize."

"Hell, us too. But we also had our rations reduced. Now, surely one of you boys is open to negotiating."

Butch was met with shrugs and nods as he gauged his group's response.

The Rebel soldier called again. "Don't toe that line."

Butch approached the river. It was a placid slow-moving stretch about twenty yards wide. The only disturbance in the water were the ripples that radiated out from the shore of each speaker, merging in small waves and settling out in all directions.

"All right," Butch said. "First things first. Name and rank there, Johnny Reb."

"Andrew J. Callowhill the first." In grand fashion, the soldier removed his cap and bowed. All smiles, his companions gave a smattering applause.

Butch flashed a grin at his men as he called, "All right, Cow-hill it is."

"That's Callowhill, sir." Callowhill never looked to his men, only smiled a picket grin. "Call-o-hill. Now, what did that old country bumpkin mother of yours come up with?"

Butch could not help but chuckle to himself as both sides broke out in laughter.

"Well, sir, if you'll know. I go by Butch—"

"Your name is Butch?" The Rebel bank laughed and clapped. Callowhill slapped his hat across his knee. "Butch might be the kind of man who'd live up on *Cow Hill*," he added.

Men on both sides cackled.

"No. I said, 'go by.'" Butch tugged at the ends of his jacket, attempting to regain his dignity with his posture.

Both banks had relaxed into a jovial scene where men milled about and made quiet conversation with one another. All heads turned back to Callowhill as he spoke. It appeared that he savored the audience.

"She must not be a creative old sheep dog, now, is she?" He perched one foot up on a driftwood log at the water's edge. He leaned an elbow on his upraised knee and held his white whiskered chin in his hand. He wobbled a bit and smiled. "Well, nice to know you, Butch. Boys, give old Butch your regards."

The Confederates on the bank mock saluted Butch, and plunked stones into the water near where he stood.

Butch spoke while leaning his rifle against a small shrub. "What is your rank, Mr. Callowhill? Lieutenant blowhard of the bummers? Last in line, are you?"

"No, sir." Callowhill raised his voice over jeers and clapping from the Union bank. "We are scouts. We've got a battalion just over yonder fit for a right and mighty fray."

With this, the Union soldiers' smiles evaporated. Unease settled over their bank.

Callowhill's genial grin collapsed flat and his eyes sharpened. Several of the men on his bank cocked the hammers of their rifles. "We are taking you as prisoners of the Confederacy," he added. "Stand up, leave your arms where they lay."

Butch stepped to his rifle, rolled his foot over a stone, and stumbled to his knees in the mud at the water's edge. All at once the Rebel bank erupted in raucous laughter.

A man fired his musket into the air, causing the Union bank to brace. The Rebel laughter amplified as Butch caked the mud from his uniform.

Callowhill turned to his men and said, "He must be a cavalry man—he ain't used to those webbed feet!"

The Union soldiers wore skeptical looks, and Butch made a settling motion with his hands.

"All right, all right," Callowhill said, calming his men. "Sorry, there Butch. We was just relieving the tension in the air." He adjusted his cap with a wide smile and continued, "We ain't scouts, but we been through the mill, Old Butch. We had our rations cut. We ain't seen hide nor hair of the battle grounds going on three weeks. We may be fighting ya'll soon enough, but we'd like to offer you some goods by means of trade. See if we can't improve our living before we go dying."

"Sure enough," said Butch. "It's been a long road for these boys."

"Sure has, Butch. Sure has. And all in three years."

More men appeared on each bank and continued to cluster around each speaker. The Union shore huddled in discussion, resulting in several men heading up and over the bank, out of sight.

Seeing this departure, several Rebel soldiers clicked their rifles into ready hands in response.

Callowhill motioned for his rifle as he spoke. "Now, what business are you pulling, Butch?"

"Not pulling a thing. Calm down, boys." Butch raised his hands, palms out. "They've gone to grab a small crate of some haberdashery that we might toss to you sorry mutts. We may need a raft and pole, so we don't have to wade to make deals."

Friends and Enemies

"Don't you cross us, Butch. We come as good, God-fearing men."

"We aren't crossing you. This water's cold. Your men willing to wade?" He tossed a small pebble toward an eddy on Callowhill's bank which poked a single hole in a thin layer of ice.

Callowhill spoke quietly to the soldiers on his bank, and they placed their muskets in teepee triads, a tension settling out of their movements. He removed his gray hat and tossed it across the stream where it landed at Butch's feet. A few Rebels now disappeared over the rise to the south.

"Where're your boys going now?" Butch lifted the hat and wiped it clean. "You dropped something."

"It's a sign of good faith, you mule. They've gone to grab some supplies worth trading." He pointed to a few of his men's hats.

Callowhill's men followed suit, sending gray hats sailing through the air. "Now, show you're good for it, Yanks."

Butch removed his hat and looked to his men for confirmation. Several blue caps drifted through the air, landing about the rocks on the other shore. A few men on either side donned the opponents' colors and pantomimed salutes to one another.

Callowhill said, "As firm as a handshake, boys." He held both his hands up, palms out to punctuate the accord, then brought them together in a single clap. "Now, we've not got many choices to offer, but we've got quantity to high heaven."

※

It was later in the afternoon now, and they'd be settling around fires for an evening meal soon. Callowhill and Butch stood at the water's edge, with their comrades seated around them listening.

61

"We're just about the opposite," said Butch. "Not much by way of quantity, but we've a good many things that might draw interest. Give us time to organize."

"Same. Same, old Butch. Don't often meet such kind fellows in these parts."

The sun began its descent as each side sent more men back to their encampments beyond the banks. Running parallel to the waterway, and crossing it a few miles downstream, was a rail line choked in the advance of the Union Army. The Yankees positioned stump seats and primitive fire rings, preparing to spend a few hours away from camp. Seeing this, the Rebels cleared a portion of their bank, fashioning seats out of large stones and driftwood as well.

The soldiers who'd left each side soon returned, all toting some supplies for bartering. The Yankees brought some small planks of wood, and a tattered Union flag darkened from gun smoke and weathering. The flagpole was a long staff with a splintered end. Slightly upstream the Union bank the men laid out the supplies and began fashioning small rafts.

Butch surveyed the lot they'd accumulated: several sacks of random supplies such as playing cards, tea, coffee, books, and a banjo.

On the Rebel shore, they produced a few small crates, as well as a harmonica and a second banjo. Nearly all of the men had removed their heavy wool coats, as the white sunlight and the geniality of the activity had warmed them up.

"Callowhill, old dog," Butch called to the Confederate bank, huddled in discussion of the value of their goods. He skipped a stone that caromed clear to the other shore where the men were standing.

"Goddammit, Butch," Callowhill hollered. "We're organizing. Write your mother a letter."

Soldiers on both sides stoked small fires using some of the driftwood along the shores. The flames jumped to life and countered what light had been receding from the banks. They ate and drank together along the banks, with the water between them serving as little inconvenience. The plucking banjos played rudimentary versions of popular songs, provoking soldiers on each side to clap and sing along.

On the edge of the water, Butch filled a pipe and puffed it against a match. He wore Callowhill's gray cap, tilted low. The dark roots of his beard were beginning to sweep and curl out away from his face. Across the stream, Callowhill's was the inverse—short, close cropped, stark white.

Someone handed Butch a rolled newspaper from Baltimore, which he tucked under his arm. He barred his teeth in a grin, gritting the end of the pipe as the smoke rose in clouds around him.

A kingfisher came fast from upstream, clicking and chirping along the water. It perched only for a moment on the Union bank, where the ship builders stirred it to flight. It swept to the Confederate side, where men appeared from the trailhead and flushed it once more. A vibrant blue contrasting the gray and white landscape, it skimmed along the water and perched in a tree above the Union soldiers sorting their goods. With darting eyes, it inspected the men one by one, then continued downstream stitching from one bank to the other as it went.

"All right, old friend," Callowhill said. "We've but two things in large number. One crate, about eight pounds of our own fine tobacco. Grown in that method you despise, but strong and flavored. The other, a heavier load for sure, of sweet-dried persimmons. We picked them ourselves in the summer. Stored them in a barn along the Rappahannock. Retrieved them not one week ago when we set up camp outside of Fredericksburg."

"Dried persimmons, there?"

"Sweeter than hell, Old Butch. Like a sweet kiss from that woman you left behind."

"We've been in hell since we marched from Pennsylvania. We're about due for some sweets." He smiled. "These southern women that hang around our camp ain't so sweet no more."

Callowhill removed a wad of chew from his lip and flung it into the water. He repositioned the blue cap and tucked his thumbs in his waistband. "Sounds like they weren't willing to trade with you either. I guess you haven't got much to offer them." His smile sharpened. "What do you say, Old Butch? Fruit and Tobacco sound appealing?"

Butch nodded to the grumblings among his men. Looking back to Callowhill he said, "It may be, depending upon the price." He removed the rolled paper from underneath his arm and flung it across the river. "We got some reading material from Baltimore and Philadelphia."

The Rebels gave little response.

"Any one among you able to read?"

The Union banjo player struck up "Dixie," the Yankees singing along in caricature accents. Soldiers on both sides laughed and jeered, tossing pebbles and branches across at one another.

The banjo and harmonica on the southern shore chimed in, and all men sang and hummed along, drawing cheers and applause. Butch retrieved a knapsack and returned to the edge of the bank. When the men settled down again, he spoke.

"We have a dozen or so ears of corn."

The Rebel soldiers voiced their approval.

Butch continued, "We have a flask of whiskey."

The Rebel cheers rose.

"Gents," Butch said, "you might be happy to hear. . . we have a bit of coffee we're willing to part with."

The Confederate soldiers hooted and hollered with joy. Their calls were echoed by their Union counterparts.

Callowhill clapped slowly with wide strokes. "Old Butch, you came through for us. We been mixing coffee with dirt for the better part of a month. We'll be sure to avoid that pumpkin head of yours if we see you at the ball."

The Union soldiers that had been working upstream produced the small rafts that they had constructed to pass the goods from shore to shore. A thin line with one end tied to a rock would be used to tug them from one side to the other. The other soldiers approached them to inspect their quick engineering. They held up the small rafts for the Confederate bank to admire.

"Well, looky here, boys," Callowhill said. "They've brought the navy!"

Now the banks were a boisterous scene. Goods passed from shore to shore, tugged along back and forth. Men drank and ate, and the conversation rose and fell with topics of politics and war. Pipe smoke mingled with the stacks climbing from the small fires. As the sun leaned against the horizon, the men donned their coats and moved in closer together on each bank.

In an effort to retrieve a shipment of tobacco, a Yankee stumbled at the shoreline and soaked his pants to the thigh. Men on both sides applauded. He regained his footing on the bank, removed his coat and untucked his uniform, and sloshed closer to the warmth of a fire. A gray coat whipped across the stream and wrapped itself around his head, nearly knocking him over once more. He turned toward the Rebels and tipped his cap.

A rebel stood from his cookfire and said, "It's a spare, but I wouldn't wear it tomorrow if I were you."

The dampened soldier swung the coat on and mock curtsied.

One side to the other offered biased accounts of conflicts, eager to hear how the opposition viewed major losses and victories. They shared joint complaints about commanding officers and politicians, laughing together as they quantified the hardships of service.

When recounting Fredericksburg, the Rebel yell swept through the Confederate bank.

"A damn shame what Burnside did to you boys,"

Callowhill said. "Kept feeding you to slaughter."

The bright fires now illuminated the shoulders of the banks. The men's faces were illuminated against the shadows of the banks as they huddled together in the cool onset of evening.

Callowhill stepped to the edge of the bank and said, "We've an interesting offer, boys."

"More tobacco!" a Yankee called.

"Now, now, boys," Butch said. "Let's hear it, Callowhill."

"We've got letters from home and the like. Even an image taken here and there. Diaries, journals, what have you. We're willing to part with them for a time. Give you something more entertaining to read than a Union paper. They got it all wrong anyway."

"We've got the same. Even an extra pair of shoes." Butch motioned to some of his men to hand him the satchel of personal effects.

A tied and wrapped bundle of envelopes was hurdled from the Confederate bank. Butch grabbed the satchel of Union belongings and with a wide swing he sent it through the air.

Callowhill read the names on the envelopes in a mock northern accent. "Smith. Here are letters from Smith's mother. O'Cleary. O'Cleary wrote quite a bit. Davids. Shea. Howe."

His men echoed the names and accent upon receiving the letters, and Butch began his roll call in a caricature of a southern tongue.

Soldiers on both sides recited passages to one another. Pockets of laughter broke out. Men read in high, feminine voices as they shared the sentiment of wives and mothers.

"We can't help but notice that your men seem to think God is on your side," Butch said. "Or so they say to their mothers. But our mothers have been telling us just the same!"

"God ain't picking sides here, Butch. A parent can't choose between the children. Mama, Papa—they wouldn't oblige."

One of Callowhill's men called out. "You boys know any term besides 'graybacks'?"

"Same as 'Yankee', boy," Butch said. "Call it a term of endearment."

A Union soldier stood atop a large rock and began reciting, "'. . . It was at that moment, Darling, when I realized how greatly I do miss that homemade apple pie!'"

Rough laughter broke out on both banks, and the banjo players were prompted to strike up the soft chords of a song called "Home Sweet Home."

A Rebel soldier stood and said with a smile, "I don't regret a sentence of that letter! Finest pie you'd ever have!"

Callowhill shook a letter above his head and the men quieted down.

"Listen. Listen, boys. This here is from Mr. Shea. Now, Mr. Shea seemed to think that there was a woman in the company of these soldiers." The Rebels cheered and whistled. "No, no, boys. A female enlisted. Hiding her identity. Mr. Shea, you care to elaborate?"

The Rebels urged Shea on, but the Yankees grew quiet on their shore.

"Shea?" Callowhill lowered the letter. "Any you boys named Shea? Know Shea?"

"Shea won't answer that call, Callowhill." Butch folded the letter he had been reading and tucked it back into the envelope. "Shea passed. Spent the night in the streets of Fredericksburg and did not see the sun rise."

"You traded us the letters of someone's darling who passed. . . ?"

"We're all someone's darling."

Both groups of men fell silent. The fires popped and hissed as the damp wood burned. Soft conversations fell into a murmur and died along the darkening banks.

"These men sent their own letters over. We said only

worth a read, then send them back." Callowhill's face was nearly blurred in the darkness. "Why send words meant for dead men?"

"You ought to just read them for sentiment."

Callowhill opened another letter and leaned against the log. Reading, he ran his fingers over the white whiskers of his beard. He called to the Union soldiers, "Howe? William Howe?"

"No sense in calling the names, Callowhill."

"Dead? Every letter?"

"Dead or missing," Butch said. "We didn't want them back. They're letters all the same when you don't know who penned them."

"How do you have so many?"

"We had a courier was killed about a week ago. We spent three days returning letters to regiments in camp. Anyone we couldn't track down is in our hands."

The wind was picking up, sweeping the water into small ripples. The rafts clustered along the Confederate bank and knocked together in the little waves of the evening winds.

"This boy Howe was going to have a baby in the spring." Callowhill sat on the log in a heap. He spoke just loud enough to be heard. "Said he felt awful sick. Lost some thirty pounds. 'Seen death behind him and in front of him,' he says. He was quiet for a moment as he read. "This son of a bitch was only ever paid four dollars for his service. Something tells me he's alive, but on the road North. I hope he is at least. Help the woman get the planting right."

"Callowhill, no sense recounting. Your men want these letters back?"

"If those men want them, keep 'em. And we'll do the same. Firm as a handshake."

The light from the fires flickered and silhouetted the men along the banks. The first few stars perforated the sky. The reflecting water was now brighter than the shorelines, an inky gleam of bending light.

"I wish them well," Callowhill said. His white beard glowing against his sun beaten face. The geniality in his voice had evaporated. "And your men here."

"Sure enough, Callowhill. We'll be sure to keep an eye out for that yellow grin."

"Honored to know you, Old Butch." Callowhill said. "Throw my hat."

The hats flocked through the night sky.

"You and your boys are the worst scouts I've ever seen," Butch said.

Dark bodies saluted the opposing shore as they made their way back to the encampments. The gray uniforms floated like ghosts until they disappeared over the bank. Some Union men still sat reading to themselves, leaning close to the fires as the deep cold of night settled in.

7

Soldier's Heart

The old farmhouse glowed in the first light. Frost on the fields leading up to it made it look like a child's dollhouse. William had been gone for months, yet the property seemed cleaner than usual without him leaving shovels and rakes leaning here and there, or half-finished construction projects propped up in the yard. "I'll be home to see the baby born," he had said. Hannah knew full well the rise of her belly had dropped. Time had nearly run out on the promise.

I don't care when you come home—I just need you to come home.

At the crest of the roof, half a dozen crows were jawing at one another. When the wind shifted the chimney smoke swirled around them as they half-opened their wings to warm up in the sunrise. They shifted their feet gently to keep them from freezing to the slate shingles. They barked their cackles back and forth.

Hannah was watching them from the outhouse. A board propped the door despite the cold wind seeping in, so she could keep an eye on her toddler daughter inside. As she sat, she reread two messages from William. This was now the only time she spent with her husband.

One note was the last letter she had received from William. The other was the planting instructions for the spring, which he had written down for her in case he hadn't returned in time. She had helped with the planting before but could not do it on her own. As she read the list, she contemplated which of the neighboring men she could enlist and wondered how to ask.

The letter placed William's regiment outside of Washington D.C. Hannah received his letter weeks after it had been written, which was around the same time that word of the Battle of Fredericksburg reached Perkiomenville, featuring mass casualties in the Pennsylvania 116th.

Other families in town had received word that men were hospitalized back in Washington. The papers told of mismanagement of the army, of sitting in camps while the Rebels reinforced the ridge, delayed construction of a bridge, and still charging into the teeth of the enemy despite the obvious disadvantages. All of this Hannah kept to herself, trying to avoid bringing it to life by sharing it with anyone in town or with the local community at church as they worked to fill the void William had left behind.

She would wake her toddler, Charles, and feed him a small meal of eggs and oats so they could get to service early to thank the older members of her community for dropping off loaves of bread and the like. A note on the door would let her know the back leg of a deer was now hanging in the spring house. In the first major snowstorm she woke up to male voices in the yard; her neighbor Jim had replenished the cordwood stacked under the porch. When she went out to retrieve a log, she saw that Jim's wife, Susan, had baked a loaf of sourdough bread wrapped in brown paper. In this way, the communities constricted around those who sacrificed the most for the war.

Before and after mass there would be social mixing, which, for several years, had involved sharing the accounts from personal letters as well as the latest news reports from the war. These conversations applied a sort of social pressure to those who hadn't enlisted. One went so far as to mail a petticoat back for those unwilling to join. Hannah wondered if that was how William eventually found the desire to make a name for himself.

"There's nothing to take personally," she had said.

Notes from a Deserter

"These young ones will carry my name. They need a name they can carry without it weighin' them down."

On cold mornings like this, she surprised herself at how proficient she was at using minimal wood to produce a strong fire. She would use pages of the newspaper to start and watch the very edges of print stretch and curl before turning into ghosts before adding more kindling. She couldn't bring herself to read the latest before committing it to flames.

Now, from the outhouse, the last little remnants of the paper leapt from the chimney and fluttered along the crow lined ridge. Between waves of nausea triggered by the infant bucking inside of her, she stacked her priorities for the day. The wind tested the integrity of the board propping the door.

She could see the top of her son's head pass one window and stop at the next, tapping on the window. A doll floated into view. Hannah waited for the nausea to pass before cleaning herself and heading back inside. The crows laughed as she matched her tracks, print for print, in the frosted grass.

A sharp clap of a door slamming brought her neighbor, Susan, running panicked in her direction. She had two children of her own in tow.

"Hannah," she cried. "Lord help, Hannah!"

As a reflex Hannah rushed herself inside to protect her toddler from the unknown. She watched the neighboring house for any signs of concern, holding the door for the rush of little ones and their mother.

The sudden excitement stirred the baby in her belly to roll over, and the nausea had her blowing gentle exhales in the doorframe. She leaned into the door and welcomed the cold wind onto the nape of her neck.

Susan greeted her by raising a shaking hand to touch her shoulder. The connection helped settle both women. "Hannah, are you well?"

"I am. I'm fine. What's happening? Are you okay?"

"Oh, I hate to bother you—I really do. Jim's in the barn again. I can't get through to him. He turned for you last time. I just want to get him into bed where I know he's safe."

"Has he got a gun?"

"I don't think so, but I haven't been able to check. We was eating breakfast. I went to oil the pan and dropped the bottle into it. It popped so loud I jumped. Well, we all jumped. Sent him shaking and hollerin'. He went under the table, talking something awful, eyes like silver dollars." Her teeth chattered with adrenaline. "All I could think was to get the kids away."

"You're fine, Susan. The kids are fine. Jim'll be all right. Let's give him a few minutes for it to pass." From the top of a hutch Hannah retrieved a small cup full of marbles. "Here kids. I need you to take these upstairs and play. Please don't come down until we come back into this house. We are going next door for some adult business."

Just like that their little feet hammered up the stairs. Hannah grabbed a coat and locked the back door while Susan waited on the porch. "Hannah," she said. "Lock them doors."

Hannah rolled the latch and grabbed her coat. They stood for a moment looking out at the neighboring property. Everything was still. The deep red barn stood in a field that glistened with frost. Looking closely, Hannah could see Jim's tracks leading up to the door.

Susan leaned her head on Hannah's shoulder. "I hate to bother you with this. I feel like I can't do this anymore. He ain't fit to live with. When he gets like that, it isn't him."

"I wish you took that gun."

"He said it was like taking his manhood away. I told him, 'You don't shoot no deer with a pistol.' He laughed and said, 'We ain't safe from no graybacks if we ain't got a gun.' Set in his ways since this war."

"He was set in his ways before, Susan. You used to say he was as stubborn as a goat."

"No, Hannah, it ain't the same. He ain't the same since the war. I hope your husband comes back. I'm awful fearful that mine never did."

As the women made their way out to the road, the crows lifted from the roof and collected in a large black walnut tree. At the sharp smack of a gunshot, they picked up again and scattered into the woodlot, cawing and carrying on.

Hannah left Susan crouched in the grass, frozen with terror except when shook by a tremor. The rising sun was turning the frost into fog. Hannah approached the barn from the shaded side, where the icy blades of grass still crunched along Jim's tracks.

She leaned against the door to listen. There was a rustle from the opposite side of the barn, and sheep trotted out into a fenced in pen. Steam rose from their warm bodies. Jim was away for the sheering last season. Now, with two years of growth, their wool was curled and knotted and covering their faces. Looking both full-bodied and sick, they were gray clouds with hooves passing into the field. Hannah looked down the side of the barn, but the owner never followed the flock.

"Jim. It's Hannah. Are you all right this morning?"

She breathed in through her nose until the baby would not allow her lungs to expand, and then exhaled and a drifting wisp of breath lifted up out of the shadow and into the light.

"Jim. I'm going to come in this barn now. I'm fixing breakfast and I want to eat with you all. I got some peanut butter from the ladies at the church. I can put it on toast for you—your favorite."

Hannah reached her hands to the back of her hips and arched her back. "You put that gun on the ground, Jim. I'm obviously bringing a baby with me."

Susan watched like a bedded deer as the great door groaned, and Hannah sidestepped into the barn.

Inside the barn was warm, insulated by the stacked stores of hay and the body heat of a resident cow named Suzy. She stood in the first stall and was unmoved by the morning's excitement. Like Hannah, Suzy was pregnant.

At the sight of Hannah, Suzy lumbered to her feet and slow-strode over to the railing, looking for a fresh tuft of hay. Hannah watched her and beyond, listening to shuffling coming from the back of the barn.

"Jim, please tell me you're all right. You in here? Safe?"

She peered down the row of stalls and caught the telltale Union Blue cap bob behind a bale of hay. To know that he was alive settled her nerves.

"Jim, I'm going to feed Suzy. Hope you don't mind."

Suzy's great heft was exaggerated even more by her pregnancy, and she gently nodded her head as she watched Hannah pull from a fresh bale. Hannah rubbed the cow's forehead and listened to the deep, muffled crunch of her chewing.

"She's such a beautiful girl, Jim. Can't wait to see who goes first, me or her. What's your bet?"

From the corner of her eye a quick shadow moved from behind one bale to another.

"No more shots, Jim. You're safe. Be safe around me and Suze."

Hannah took exaggerated breaths as she made her way down the stalls, letting Jim know she was approaching. The back of the barn opened up into an open space with a hay loft above. The stacks limited the incoming light and darkened the space. Jim's shaking legs gave him away, hiding behind a wagon load of manure.

"Let it pass Jim. I'm here when you need me."

A feed bag made a perfect squat stool for the pregnant

woman. She took a moment to admire Jim's organization of his supplies. Hay bales bone dry and evenly stacked, feed bags cinched tight, and all the seed bags for the spring piled beside the arsenal of manual tools for the sowing.

"Jim, listen—if you can hear me. I've been thinking about planting. William left me some instructions, but I can't do it alone. I can certainly help some, but I'll be nursing."

As her eyes adjusted, she could see a mass lying near the open stable door. At first it looked like a person hiding under a wool blanket, moving slightly but trying to remain hidden. It dawned on her that it was a sheep. She could see its blood-wet face, and the death throes had tangled it in hay and scat. It lay halfway in the field, halfway in the barn, yawning into the sunlit grass.

Hannah kept her eyes on the sheep as she spoke. "Oh, Jim, now you've done it. You're going to need to process this sheep in time for William." A winced smile squeezed a tear to roll down her cheek.

His voice trembled. "He come back?"

"No, no, he's not back," she wiped her cheek, "he's as good as on his way. And a lamb steak on the table would be the perfect way to welcome him home. D'you agree?"

The legs under the wagon bent and he sank to a crouch. She could see now that the service revolver was lying on the ground. Jim shook as he sobbed. Another sheep poked its head back into the barn and nibbled at the woolen hay of the corpse.

"I'm sorry, Hannah. Where's Susan and the kids? Did I scare her off?"

"They're fine."

"It comes on so quick—"

"Jim, they're fine. And so are you. Now let's get this cleaned up."

He turned his attention to the dead sheep. "I came in the barn, and she was the first thing I seen. She was gray—all gray. I don't know what all came over me. Like a nightmare but a memory, too"

Soldier's Heart

Hannah approached the wagon and stood where Jim could look up at her. She smiled and bent to pick up the revolver. The full scent of manure nearly knocked her over. She scurried to the open door and retched in the grass.

Jim walked Hannah home. The sunlight warmed their backs and loosened the frozen gravel beneath their feet. They discussed William's planting instructions as they surveyed both properties. Hannah listened as he explained a collaborative planting project between the two properties.

"This might be our chance to try it."

"We'll see what William has to say about it," Hannah insisted.

Jim went on to explain how Hannah and Susan could prioritize the animals, increase the chicken flock, and he could use the Howe's mules to increase the plowed land on both properties. "More work will be good for me," he concluded. "It'll keep my mind from wanderin'."

Susan had gathered the children on the porch. They welcomed him home all over again. As they made their way inside the Howe's, Hannah stayed for a moment on the porch. She imagined her own husband's return, any day now or never. She called inside, "I'm going to use the latrine then I'll come help with breakfast."

In the walk back to the outhouse she lowered her restraint and let the emotions rush on. The wind had bite to it, but the sunrise was a glowing reminder at how temporary the cold season was. The trees hid their ice on their western faces as the golden fans stretched long into the fields, hinting at what spring could be.

The crows picked their conversation up once again, drawing Hannah's attention back to the neighboring barn. She could see they had landed in the sheep's pen, hopping in and out of the bands of light. They goaded one another on with caws like raspy jeers. Hannah watched as one mounted the fallen sheep and kneaded at the overgrown wool with its claws.

The sheep had fallen face first into the sunlit field. The blood drew the crow's attention, warm and sticky. It explored the taste with clicks of its beak. A sharp lance at the sheep's eye drew the others onto the corpse, laughing as they went.

Hannah wrung her frown like wet laundry. With her neighbors in her house, she could close the latrine door and have a short moment to herself.

8

Runaways

John couldn't hold his breath any longer, but he didn't struggle as his brother held him underwater. The river was cool in the early fall, but the air was cooler. The riverbed was sandy, with the granules kicking up into clouds in the small pool.

The hand over his head moved to tug on John's ear. He emerged in a bed of weeds in a small eddy, suppressing coughs as his lungs re-inflated. His eyes were wide and reddened. He mouthed, "They gone?"

A soft whisper in response. "They gone."

Moses pressed his back against the bank and craned his neck to survey their surroundings. John caught him suppressing a small grin as he turned his head to look upstream.

"Were they upstream there, or over by the carriage road?"

Moses' face remained facing upstream.

"How many did you actually see?"

John could see Moses' cheek flex, hiding his smile.

"They coming back," Moses said. He reached his hands to the back of John's head and forced his face into the water.

John wrapped his arms around Moses' legs and swept him into the river. He climbed onto his brother's back, pushing him headfirst into the murky water. Reaching for the exposed roots on the bank, John pulled himself up. Moses floated limp, mimicking a dead drift. He rolled over and floated on his back, his teeth pearls against his tawny clay skin and the muddied water.

79

"How you going to joke about that?" John cleared his nose one nostril at a time as he took a seat on the ledge of the bank.

"You the one drowning me."

"You weren't drowning." John wiped his face with the crux of his elbow. "You said white folks were coming."

"I'm always hearing white folks. Every preacher I ever heard was white."

"I knew you were going to get me killed. I never should've let you talk me into running." John removed his shirt and wrung it out. "I ain't even believing we're true brothers."

Moses emerged from the stream and sat beside him. "Now why'd you go and say a hurtful thing like that?"

"All Master Scott ever said about you, is that we was bought on the same day."

"Oh, John Dent. I look at you and it's like looking in a mirror."

"Well, that must be an ugly side of me."

Moses blew the water out of his nostrils. "We're better off already. Planting season's started."

The leaves had begun to sprout, and the forest was losing lines of sight. Grasses emerged along the mottled banks. The April sun was rising, coaxing everything awake. A flock of geese paddled its way downstream, plucking roots from the aquatic plants along the bank.

Moses spoke like he was giving the body of water its name for the first time, overpronouncing the words as he wagged his finger at each syllable, "This here is the Chesapeake Bay. I came here before when Master Scott was seeing his aunt in Pennsylvania."

"How could you know a thing like water just by looking?"

"Master Scott stayed at a hotel just up here. I slept out in the stable with the horses. The stable buck told me all about this water, mixed freshwater and salt."

"And here we are." John motioned to the edge of the water.

"And here we are."

The sun was rising warm, and fog billowed out of the riverbed. Distant pops and the rolling thunder of cannons sounded in the distance. The two fell silent, listening to the barrage.

"Can't wait to be north of the fighting," John said. "How far do you think we've gone?"

Moses paced over and looked back the way they came, then met John beside the water. "About fifty miles since we saw your sign, I'd say."

"I don't know what I'm running from more, Master Scott or his signs."

"*'John Dent. $100. A genteel Negro and pleasant when spoken to.'* He misses you."

John shrugged, "I don't know if it said all that."

"I wonder what my signs say," Moses said. "'Good worker,' I bet. I'm the best damn worker my master's ever seen. He'll miss me this season, I'm sure."

"Lord willing," John said.

"Lord willing."

Moses removed his shirt and wrung it as John had done. "Makes no matter. At this point, we're better off dead than ever going back. Not got much choice." He removed his trousers, wrung them, and lay them in a pool of light as a shiver rode the scars along his spine. They crisscrossed like the markings on a butcher's block. The brightening sky above him darkened Moses into a silhouette.

"We've had no choice since the moment we left." Moses waded into the water. "But I'm better off dead than on a farm."

John hung his head, unable to disagree. He leaned forward to have a drink from the brackish water. He spat it out.

"We'll be free men in two days' time," Moses said. He strode through the water, cupping chilled handfuls against himself.

John washed his face at the bank. "First thing we need is a proper meal. I'm so hungry I could eat damn near anything."

"We'll come upon something small today," said Moses. "Tonight, we'll make it through to a conductor in Baltimore. They have some food about."

They had been on the run for several days and hadn't stopped since the previous afternoon, when an elderly groundskeeper wielding a rake chased them from their cover in a church barn. John reclined on the bank and closed his eyes. He listened to Moses hum as he bathed himself. Songbirds flitted around them, hitting the mayfly hatch emerging from the water. Cannon fire rose up far away, with a soft crackle of musket fire underneath. The water was smooth and steaming, blurring the landscape in a rising fog that merged with the rolling smoke from the battlefields. The geese were close now, honking to each other while paddling in and out of the currents swirling in the eddy.

Moses returned to the bank and pulled on his pants. "I need a rest." He reclined next to his brother.

John was scanning in the direction of the fighting. "Well, we sure as hell ain't staying here."

Moses closed his eyes and let his limbs go limp.

"Moses, we ain't resting here."

John stood up. "Let's go."

Moses grinned as John nudged him in the ribs, but he kept his eyes closed and his arms resting at his side.

"Goddammit, Moses—"

A loud hacking cough cut into the streamside. The foliage on the opposite bank rustled as a head bobbed through the undergrowth, then dipped and made its way to the water's edge.

The runaways read each other's faces. They rolled flat on their chests and crawled into the brush. A figure stepped out, flushing the geese into a honking flight up around the bend. From a distance he looked gaunt. His tattered Union Blues hung large and stiff like the tattered clothes of a scarecrow.

He coughed again and stood staring at the water. He dropped to an unsteady knee and drank from the stream. The salt in the water made him spit it out, too. After rinsing his face, he collapsed onto his side.

From the reeds on the opposite bank, the brothers could hear the deep grunting of either suppressed coughing or sobbing.

Moses whispered, "Playing possum."

John remained fixed on the soldier; his mouth open to silence his rushed breathing.

The man rolled over and his bent knees flopped together with a thud. He curled into a fetal position, wincing as if gut shot.

"He's wearing blue." Moses rolled onto an elbow. "No rifle and hardly any supplies."

Another series of coughs surged through the man's body, deep and hacking. He rocked back and forth in pain.

"He's wounded," Moses said. "Let's get the hell away from him."

"We're far enough away from the fighting. He wasn't wounded then wandered some miles to this place." John watched the trail where the soldier had come from. "He's got to be a deserter."

Dry heaving hacks broke heavy into the morning air.

"That man needs help," John said.

"Not ours."

"Ain't he fighting for us?"

"Everyone is a threat to us. We need to get upstream. We'll loop around on the other side of that hill." Moses cocked his head in its direction. "He'll never even know we were here."

The man lay motionless.

John looked over his shoulder at the subtle trails leading into the safety of the trees.

Moses rose to a crouch and reached for his shirt. In an exhale he said, "You ready?"

"This man needs help. Maybe he could help us, too."

"You've lost your mind."

"He could never capture us. He's ill. He couldn't split kindling."

Moses stared at the soldier. He shook his head in a soft rhythm that increased when his eyes met John's.

"No. Now you follow me." He began to make his way into the forest in perfect silence.

John instead took long soft strides through the water to keep from startling the soldier. He took note of the trail that the man emerged from to reassure himself that the soldier had come alone. As he approached, he could hear low sobbing and labored breathing.

The trail was well used on this side of the river, and the soldier rested beside a pile of timbers that had been stacked beside the stream.

John reached for the pistol tucked in the man's belt and tossed it aside.

"You all right now? You shot?"

The soldier curled into a ball.

John crouched and spoke in a soft tone. "No, no. I'm not aiming to hurt you."

The soldier rolled to face John and recoiled. "You stay away," he said. "Get away."

"Now calm down. I was just making sure you all right."

"For Christ's sake, stay away."

John rocked back to the seat of his pants to show he was no threat. He sat positioned between the soldier and his pistol.

The man was pale and sweat-soaked with a patchy beard. His shirt, weighed down and draping his shoulders in sweat, was encrusted with dirt and vomit.

The soldier looked to see Moses reluctantly re-entering the stream, then again at John.

"I've got nothing to do with you." His yellow skin was fading green, and the sickly aroma of urine and excrement hung in the air around him. He was thin to the point of appearing starved.

"Have you been shot, sir?"

"Just let me be."

Stepping onto the bank, Moses hissed an echo of the man's words. "Let him be, John. Let's just go."

"Have you been shot? Is the fighting that near to here?"

The soldier stared at John for a moment, then looked past him to the pistol.

"I haven't been shot," he said.

"Well, what's all the fuss?"

Moses knelt at the edge of the bank, wringing out his shirttail while standing watch.

"I've been sick," the soldier said.

"You heading to a doctor?"

"I tried to see the doctor."

"You look like hell."

Another coughing fit took the man. To break it, he crawled to the water's edge and cupped more water to his mouth. Moses nodded to the gun, which John picked up and tucked into the waist of his pants. The fighting in the distance had died down after the consistent morning fray.

When he could, the man spoke.

"Are you runaways?"

"Only for a little while," Moses said.

The soldier looked at him for a moment, then dipped his hands and rinsed his face and neck.

"Get going. I don't want anything to do with you."

John ignored his demand. "Are you a runaway?"

"Get—get," the man said.

Moses stood to leave. "Shoot him," he said.

"What the hell are you talking about?"

"Use the pistol."

"He's wearing Union colors."

"If he found us sick on a bank, he'd leave us for dead, John."

John crouched nearer to Moses and spoke in a tempered voice. "He's no harm to us."

Moses reiterated the danger of staying in one place for too long, especially around white folks of any colored uniform. "Shoot him," he said.

"We left our master, but not the commandments." John stood and scanned the area around them, moving closer to the soldier.

"I'll give you what food I have," the soldier said. "But leave me my gun and be on your way."

The brothers read each other's face for a moment.

John placed the gun on the ground as a sign of goodwill.

The man crawled to the shrub line and produced a small pack. He removed tattered envelopes and placed them on the ground. He then produced something wrapped in a cloth.

"Now, what's he got?" Moses continued to scan both sides of the waterway. "We can find food somewhere else, John."

"Take it. They aren't appetizing, but they're an easy shot."

The man handed the wrap to John, who unfolded it to find a large black bird that had been partially plucked at the breasts and charred over the fire.

John furled his brow and handed the parcel back to the man. "You can't eat crows. They aren't worth a shit in terms of eating."

"Damn right we aren't eating no goddamn crow," Moses said. "John Dent, we need to get the hell out of here."

"It's not a crow. It's a cowbird."

"It's all black with that beak," John said. "Looks like a little crow to me."

"You don't even know what you're looking at." The soldier wrapped it back up and returned it to his bag.

"That's why you're sick. How long have you been surviving on food that's unfit?"

"What the hell do you know about fit foods?"
"What else is in the bag?"
"Letters."
"You a courier for the Union?"
"No. Just trying to send word I'm on my way."

Moses finally spoke to the solider. "Where?"

"Pennsylvania." Saying his destination out loud seemed to soothe the man.

When he asked Moses theirs, Moses responded only, "Somewhere free."

"Well, sir, it isn't fresh to keep a bird like that," John said. "That's poor game."

The man dunked a cloth in the stream and placed it behind his neck. "Poor game," he said. He reclined against the timbers with his pack under his head and closed his eyes. "I'm William. On my way to Pennsylvania."

Moses watched him lay back and shook his head. "Well, William, I've had about enough. John Dent, I'll be waiting for you upstream." Moses stood tall and stepped into the water.

A loud crack cut into the opening and rattled in short echoes down the stream. The soldier curled into a crouch. John grabbed for the pistol and sought cover in the nearby brush. "Moses," he called as his brother dived into the stream.

For a moment the clearing was empty except for William and the smoke from a single shot rising in a small plume.

Dogs came yelping. In an instant, they bounded onto the bank, growling and barking as William reached for a stick and tried to beat them back.

The pool where Moses had entered the stream was now clouded with sediment and red pigment swirling. The dogs flushed John from the brush as their owner arrived at the end of the trail.

"Stay where you are!" He scanned the water as he reloaded. "Sit still a while or I'll shoot again."

He was a heavy-set man, with a tiny smoking flint lock pistol. He wore adornments of wealth, from his black-leather knee-high boots to the exotic feathers pluming from his hat. The brim swung out and cast a deep masking shadow over his eyes.

"A Union soldier and two Negroes? What business brings you to my property?"

William took to his feet but did not speak. John remained behind him, as if he could recede into the brush unseen. Moses emerged from the water on the opposite bank, injured.

"Get over here or I'll kill them both," the landowner called to Moses. He obeyed, though he was hobbled by the pellet in his thigh.

"Are these runaways?" he asked.

"They are."

Moses writhed in pain, muttering, "We should have shot him."

"They didn't hurt you none?" The landowner spoke with a casual tone as he added another lead shot to the barrel. "You look a mess."

"I'm sick, sir."

"You sure you aren't running with these boys? You seem awful cozy in their company."

William's jaw clenched tight; the muscle twitched under his patchwork beard. "No."

"You better explain yourself, friend."

"I overheard them discussing their route." He stood up and contained a cough, returning to silence as if he'd said enough.

"And?" The landowner crossed his arms.

"Some plantation owner down South is willing to pay for their return, I'd bet. They look fit enough, except of course for the one you just wounded."

"Now, I didn't see you at first, friend. And I didn't want them getting away none, either."

"Well, he's wounded." William suppressed a cough again, cleared the mucus from his throat, and spat into the stream.

"What brings you so far from the fighting?"

"I'm a courier for the Union Army."

"Are you, now?"

William kneaded the sweat building on his forehead and nodded.

The landowner tracked his every movement. "Where you heading to?"

"That wouldn't make me a good courier."

"You don't seem like you're in a hurry, holding with these Negroes."

"I've delivered my accounts."

The landowner nodded to himself, trying to read the disheveled man before him.

William, forcing his shoulders broad, turned and faced upstream in defiance of the landowner's gaze.

"I'm fixing to build a bridge across here," the landowner said. "I've got a few of these logs that need split."

"Sounds like you'll need to hire some men." William picked up his bag readying to leave.

"If you split these logs with them Negroes, I'll load you in my wagon and take you into town. Save you some time on your trip. Get you a meal."

"One's injured and there're no supplies."

John helped Moses to his feet, stirring the dogs back to a growl. The landowner leveraged against the leashes. A deep red stain radiated from Moses' thigh as he stood.

"I have a wagon just over by the road," the landowner said. He had lowered his gun in compliance with casual conversation. "Won't take more than two hours. Then I'll ride you into town, turn them in, and we'll split the bounty. Then you go on your way."

"Splitting those logs is tough work. I'm in no state to—"

"What's in the wagon, sir?" John asked.

The landowner snapped, "You let us handle this, boy."

William's pale face flushed red.

"I've got some wedges and mauls that I brought for this very task."

William looked over to John and Moses, and neither could tell if it was an act or a negotiation.

He spoke without turning to face the landowner. "Get the wagon."

The landowner showed a smug grin, proud of his bargaining. "My, you do look terrible, friend."

He tucked his pistol into his belt under the bulge of his stomach. He stood without moving for a moment, looking at the haggard man and the two slaves. "Maybe after turning them in, you ought to see the doctor in town."

"Possibly."

John knelt beside Moses, both their heads down.

The landowner turned with a chuckle and started toward the wagon.

Another sharp crack rang out. The landowner winced and reached for the small of his back.

The dogs pulled the leashes free from the landowner and ran barking down the bank after some phantom game.

William ducked from the shot, then fully crumpled to the ground when John struck him from behind with a river stone. As Moses removed the landowner's pistol, John tucked the soldier's satchel under his arms.

Two men were left on the bank, one writhing and the other seemingly fast asleep beside the logs that needed to be split.

9

The Perkiomenville Hotel

The long dusk of summer and the early blue night washed the stone edifice of the *Perkiomenville Inn* with soft colors. The creek ran along steep cutoff banks, a deep-set oil painting that hemmed the base of a rocky hillside that formed the hump where the inn stood. Huge, mottled sycamores haunted the banks in the dusk. A black farm cat with white paws tried to pick its way along the bank as a string of geese honked at her from the water's edge. Two men watched them swim into the purple ribbons up the creek.

One was a tall, thin man who stood holding the halter chains he'd removed from the horse. They hung from his hand nearly to the ground, making his awkward arms appear even longer. As his companion closed the back hatch on their small, enclosed wagon, the tall man spoke softly. His eyes darted around for anyone who may overhear.

"Jesus, Mike," he whispered. "We're awful close to his house to be stopping for a drink. This is right near where he lives. He's bound to catch wind."

Bending over against the swell of his belly to check the wheel locks, Mike spoke casually in veiled meanings, his voice clear to anyone within earshot.

"Now, Abraham, we have earned a drink. You know this area well—I don't have to tell you. These fine folks will give us a sip and send us on our way. Eisenberry will be here shortly. He said to meet here tonight. Just hope the weather holds off."

Abe continued in a whisper, "And don't you think this wagon is givin' us away?"

"Don't see how so. Not the first time I've carted this wagon around. The Germans down in this valley meet here and barter grain and cigars. It's not the first they've seen." He straightened up and lowered his voice. "You think a deserter is going to ride side saddle into custody? We need a means of holding him."

Tall and nervous, Abraham nodded and opened his mouth in a silent laugh, feigning comfort. His face was long with extra skin hanging off like the head of a turkey, and his eyes tracked to the steep hillside behind the tavern.

"I just feel like I'm being watched," he said. "Just uneasy about this whole thing."

"Abe, calm yourself. This is where Eisenberry said to meet. We agreed to wait 'til dark. In just a few hours you'll be back home to the wife having done a good deed. And a good fifteen dollars in your pocket. Your namesake will thank you. Boy, look how them clouds are just piling up."

Short and stocky, Mike crossed in front of Abe, who took one last look at the hillside where the boulders in the forest were blue and crouching like men. They removed their hats and entered the hotel.

Outside, the hotel had been raised from the Pennsylvania field stone that lay scattered throughout the Perkiomen Valley. Inside, the floor, furniture, bar, and even the planks across the ceiling were all courtesy of the thinned-out forests. A small cooking fire burned in a large fireplace at the far end of the great room, and small rough-cut tables were scattered here and there for the patrons. A few older men huddled around a table in the corner, smelling of livestock and arguing prices of grain in German. They hardly noticed the newcomers pull out stools along the bar and remove their coats. Abe avoided eye contact as Mike waved and grinned.

The barkeep had a subtle German accent and sharp features rounded by a pale, graying beard. He raised an eyebrow, his face welcoming and genial. "Evening, gentlemen. What brings you in?"

"Evening," said Mike. "We'll start off with a drink." He hung his coat over his stool and sat, unbuttoning his tight vest. "Just waiting for a friend of ours."

"Good, good," the barkeep said. "What's your drink? We have whiskeys, hard cider, gin, rum, brandy, ale—cigars, too if you're interested. Gottshalk cigars. Made and rolled right across the street."

Abe spoke, "A glass of whiskey will do well." He rolled his lips into a smile with one long arm outstretched and resting on the bar, the other bent at the elbow which was perched on the seatback.

"Two whiskeys, then." Mike placed a coin on the table. "Might take a cigar for the road."

"Two whiskeys to start, then." The bartender wiped his moist hands on his pants and extended a handshake. "Isaac, Isaac Raahn."

"Mike Wagner. Pleasure."

Abe bowed his head. "Abe. Bertolet."

Isaac took note of the surname Wagner and volleyed it back with the German pronunciation. "Wagner. Are you from the old country, then?"

"Oh, no, no." Wagner grinned. "I'm a native." He chuckled. "My line's been here quite a while."

As Isaac turned his back, he called to the locals in their native tongue. He disappeared into a back room and returned accompanied by a young boy, both carrying as much ale as they could, clinking their way to the back table. Their conversation was becoming more animated, punctuated with bouts of loud laughter. They were close in around a table. Each man was darkened from soil and sunburn, and every one of them sported their choice of ragged looking facial hair.

Wagner looked over his shoulder at the men and turned to whisper a comforting word to Abe. "Howe's German, too. His name don't sound it much—he softened it at some point. Has a different spelling to it than his old man."

Abe whispered through his teeth. "How long's he been on the go?"

"December. Fredericksburg."

As Isaac reappeared with the two whiskeys, the young boy disappeared into the back. Again, Isaac barked something to the locals that neither visitor could follow. Short direct phrases, nothing to smile about.

Looking past the two visitors to the farmers, the bartender listened intently to the chatter that was picking up within the group.

Out of the corner of his eye, he now directed his conversation to the two men at the bar. "Whereabouts you from?"

Mike sipped the whiskey. His eyes squinted and his lips pursed as he swallowed. "I'm from up over the hill in New Hanover. A few, six, seven miles or so."

"New Hanover? Nice rolling hills to plant up there without all these damned boulders. We're getting down into the valleys and ridges over here. Boulders everywhere."

Mike chuckled. "Never did like living in rough countryside such as this. Seen my share of it in the army."

Abe spoke from honest memory, "I miss living in the farm country. I've been roaming too much lately."

And where are you from, Herr Abraham?"

A rush of nerves froze Abe for a moment, and he proceeded to choose his words carefully. "I'm right over in Obelisk."

"I know Obelisk well. You have a nice church in Obelisk. When I visit some of my relations over that way I can see your steeple. A white steeple."

"That's the one."

"So, what's got you roaming so much?" Isaac stood for a moment with both hands bracing the counter.

Abe took an extended drink. He coughed, returning the glass to the bar. Isaac's eyes never left him.

"I served the Union."

"Did you now?" The question settled without a

response. "You know, we have only a few in Perkiomenville who've served." Isaac stepped out from behind the bar and added one last interjection into the back conversation. "I'm cooking up some stew for the boys over there. Let me know if you want any. It's a meal that'll hold you over 'til lunch tomorrow. Venison, carrots, onions, potatoes. Hot on the fire. A few loaves of bread to go along with it." He checked the large black cooking pot in the fireplace and then disappeared once more into the back.

Mike rested his eyes on Abe for an extended stare.

Abe prodded at his glass with his fingers as long as talons.

※

The hardy stew was delicious, and, as if a dinner bell had been struck, a crowd of younger farm hands wandered into the tavern and took up the tables next to the older men. The locals in the back began their narratives again. Amidst the raucous laughter, Issac tended to their empty mugs as if he were trying to keep a leaking tub filled with ale.

Whiskey had cured Abe of both his social discomfort and the subsequent pressure of his role. Mike stooped over his steaming bowl, his wide cheeks and stout cartoonish nose reddened. Cigar smoke curled round every lantern.

In between bites and drinks, Mike shared a safe story of one of the few times he had hunted as a boy. He slow stalked a deer through a grove of oaks and tall laurel. Cresting a ridge, he shot at a blur of dark brown that flashed before him. The first deer he ever killed was a turkey.

"When it came out in the stew, my father said, 'This venison tastes like poultry!'"

The story had Abe laughing in short, high-pitched clucks that drew the attention of the room. The room quieted around them. The local men paused their conversation, the farmhands, all red in the cheeks, peeked up from their mugs at the visitors.

Isaac returned to Mike and Abe with fresh whiskeys in his hands.

Mike lowered his voice in respect. "Who threw water on their fire?"

Isaac looked at the farmers as he spoke.

"Today we received news that one of ours died in battle a few days ago."

Abe's face softened in consolation for his new friend. "Sorry to hear, Isaac. Sorry to hear." He reached his lanky arm across the bar, and patted Isaac's shoulder with his long, flaccid hand. "Where?"

Isaac's genial disposition evaporated. Only his eyes moved to turn his attention to the two visitors. "Doesn't matter." He spoke with sharp words. "That goddamned war has nothing to do with us, up here. But we're paying an awful toll for it."

"Oh, I disagree." Mike wiped his mouth with the palm of his hand. "It affects all of us—every one of us, that's for sure." With his thumb and middle finger, he slowly turned his glass as he spoke. "But I'm thankful your friend served for the Union." He grew bold. "Is he the first you lost in this town? Other towns around here have lost lots more. Dozens, even."

"We haven't dozens to offer," Isaac said.

Abe watched as the two men studied each other. Mike fought to sober a dulled wit; Isaac tried to read it.

Isaac turned away when a woman appeared in the back doorway speaking in German. The small boy trotted in beside her, red faced and panting. Mike focused on her foreign tongue, trying to decipher where one word ended and the next began. Out of a tangled mouthful of vowels and consonants he plucked one specific syllable, 'Howe', and there again a tangle that was indecipherable to him.

Isaac had offered his first tell. At the utterance of the name, he whipped a washcloth from his shoulder to the bar top as he motioned the woman and the boy out of the room in low Germanic grunts.

Perkiomenville Hotel

The other patrons had returned to their lubricated conversations. Mike looked to Abe to confirm what he had heard, but Abe was drunk. His attention was stolen away by the old German men and their stories that he couldn't hope to follow. His mouth hung open as he listened, and when they laughed, he laughed along with them.

Abe turned to Mike. "You know, honestly, I was never much of a hunter. It always seemed so much easier raising an animal than chasing one down."

Isaac stepped out from the back room and spoke only a few, efficient words in German. All at once the younger men stood and filed out of the tavern, sobered by their orders. The older men ignored the departure, unless they had said their goodbyes in unfamiliar ways that Mike and Abe had missed.

Isaac ignored that his cover had been blown. "Well, friends, would you like a room for the night?"

"No sir, I don't believe we would." There was a long pause, and a smile crept onto Mike's face.

"I suppose your friend isn't coming?"

Abe awoke from a stupor to announce, "Then we'll pick him up on the way."

"Where abouts are you heading?" Isaac removed their empty glasses from the bar top. "It's dark."

Mike produced a wrinkled fold of bills. "Not quite sure." As he counted out a rough amount, the young men's horses rattled and trotted by the open windows along the back wall.

"It's been a pleasure, Isaac. But we must be on our way."

Abe still tried to maintain an air of politeness, half waving as he followed Mike out the door.

The coolness of night had set in, and as Abe climbed up onto the wagon, he had to take deep breaths of fresh air to maintain balance. The slight taps of a drizzling rain pattered the leaves of the trees above him. He had not noticed the dark figure of Eisenberry, who had been waiting for

Notes from a Deserter

them outside. He blended into the night, wearing a Union Blue coat and tilted cap. His mustache had the ragged nature of a child's haircut.

Mike hurried along on his stout legs to the back of the carriage. "Where in the hell were you?"

"Right where I said I'd be, right when I said I'd be. What the hell are the two of you doing?"

Mike untethered the reins from the hitching post. "We said we'd meet at night—dark."

"I said *midnight*." Eisenberry marched around the back of the wagon to peer in at Abe. "*Midnight*, Mike. Unbelievable. Is he even in a state to remember which house is Howe's?"

Mike focused on his work untangling the reins of the horse and wagon. "Well, we've spooked them. No way around it, now. We need to get to him before he's flushed out."

Eisenberry returned to his horse, mounted it, trotted to the back where he could toss a canteen to Abe. "You need to shut that damn wagon door. Sure they noticed it as soon as you pulled up."

As Mike rounded the door open, the heavy wood clipped his shoulder almost knocking him to the ground. He looked in at Abe who was slouched into the corner of the bench seat, taking in deep mouthfuls of fresh air. "Get up on top of the wagon, Abe. This damn rolling cupboard is where we're going to stuff Howe when we get him. Get up in the carriage seat and get some fresh air."

As their carriage pulled out from the hotel, the stream prattled and murmured in the dark. A bodiless goose honked and splashed, then flew away invisible. From the front porch of the Perkiomenville Hotel, Isaac stood in silhouette watching them set off on a clumsy pursuit in the rain.

It was easy for Eisenberry to see where the tavern

guests had fled, even in the dark. The rain-coated dusty ruts yielded clear tracks. The road was worn muddy as it bottle-necked through the little village before dipping low at a stream crossing, then tunneling into a dense stand of tulip poplar and oak. Wagner held the reins of the wagon with Eisenberry at a trot beside them.

A bell sounded from the darkness along the broad hillside. It was the deep chime of a farmhouse bell that rattled among the trees before spreading out into the night air.

"They're warning him," Eisenberry called. "But I've a plan. We just need to get up there. He'll be waiting."

Riding on the carriage, Abe outstretched his long arms and grasped the frame of the carriage seat. "How could they know—?" He took a deep breath, then held his chin low. "They've not been gone five minutes."

"Old Isaac knew exactly who we were. Remember that boy in the bar?"

"I think that goddamned Isaac poisoned me," Abe said. "He slipped turpentine in my drink, or something." He choked down something rising in his throat. "I don't know if I've got this in me."

They rounded the horses through a bend that straightened to the direction of where the bell had rung, the road rising uphill to where the tree line gave way to a patchwork of farmsteads.

Abe shook his head and took another deep breath as a stern expression settled over him. "What the hell kind of name is Isaac, anyway?"

Mike remained focused on the road as it climbed uphill, runoff now funneling down through the wheel ruts ahead of them.

"I'll wound this son of a bitch myself if I have to. When we get there, grab the pistols from the back and pin that badge on. You better pull yourself together before we get where we're going." The mix of alcohol and adrenaline gave Mike a sort of concentrated joy in his expression. "This whole hill knows what's coming."

The wooden wagon knocked and rattled against the steep turn as a second bell, this time further up the hill, chimed in a high, sharp pitch.

The steepening road forced the horse to sink low into each stride, laboring the wagon up and through the rocky terrain. With the pace slowed, Mike took note of how fresh the trails were along the road. The rims of deep wet ruts glowed in swerving and crossing lines.

At the top of the rise the wood line broke into a rugged plateau of fields where small farms had been carved out of large stands of chestnut, oak, and tulip poplar. The farmhouses themselves were all made of stacked stone, peering out from the darkness with candlelit eyes.

Mike said, "His house is a little stone farmhouse like these, offset in a clearing of fields. That son of a bitch will be waiting for us. Bet your ass. You going to be sure which one?"

Abe wiped his face and peered out, nodding.

Eisenberry kept his horse at a trot just in front of the wagon, focused on some distant point that had yet to materialize.

"He'll know we're coming," Mike said. "He'll know."

The next two houses appeared all but abandoned, offering no sign of occupancy other than the deep, rich tone of a farm bell that radiated out from the larger of the two upon the wagon passing by. The horses pressed on. The ringing receded back into the night.

"That wagon there was at the inn," Abe said, inspecting an upcoming lot. He pressed a canteen to his lips and tilted it high in between jolts of the wagon wheels.

A house stood proud of a gentle grade ahead of them. Along the road, a stacked stone wall fenced in a flock of sheep that had been stirred up by the metallic throbbing of the bells. Tied to a post on the front porch of the house was the shadow of a horse hitched to a small hay-wagon.

As they passed the house, a sharp bell rang out. It was of a slightly higher pitch and rang frantically, without any of the rhythm that had softened out the others. A shadow darted from the bell post, small and quick as a fox.

"That boy," Mike said, and Abe remembered that small boy, with his flushed cheeks and deep breathing. He had reappeared behind the bar with Isaac.

Ahead on the road the hill crested into the shoulder of a hillside, where great clearings had been farmed beside large standing timber. Eisenberry slowed well before a short home sulking under a large black walnut tree on a corner plot. The fields behind it were hardly more than meadows; scattered crops were encroached by a healthy stand of oaks that stood like pillars of shadow through the rain.

Two outbuildings slouched in a muddied pasture. Two mules, awakened by the bells, had their chests against the fence rail. One window on the squat building radiated the light of a candle. Eisenberry's horse slowed and pivoted. The wagon rattled to standstill along the roadside where a stack stone wall was punctuated by a large limestone boulder.

A soaking Eisenberry approached the cart on Abe's side. "Well, Abe, you got enough sense to say whether or not this Howe's place?"

"It is. This is Howe's farm."

Inside the house, Howe was at the back of the room clutching his infant, eyes wide. His wife Hannah was in a panic with no outlet. She was scrunching her evening gown in fistfuls and releasing it while rubbing her knees. Their older son, Charles, sat between his mother's knees. He remained quiet in the face of the unknown danger.

At a start, Hannah rushed to the front window. "They're here, Bill." She lowered her voice and spoke again, "They're here. Oh god, they're here."

"Take the baby". He passed the baby to his wife and reached into the dark corner and retrieved a rifle. He held the rifle in the same manner as the baby, one handed against his chest. For a moment all four of them studied the windows that glowed in reflection of the candlelight, with the rain tapping on the outside and dripping beads down the panes.

Hannah's teeth chattered with adrenaline. Her husband had been home for nearly six months. She had doubted his reasons for leaving to enlist, but she came to understand it upon his return. The war had aged him, matured him, changed him in ways that took time for her to sort out. The soldier's stipends never came, but there was a new wealth that Howe brought to the family. She saw it in the ways people approached him, but also in the way he carried himself within the community. There was something unspoken now between William and her father that showed in simple things like a handshake or a disagreement. In seeing distant parts of the country and considering the ideas of many different people, he had been educated in a way he never would have known had he stayed. Her father marveled at the perspective he now offered, even if it was something the old William would have said.

His first week back she had still been at the end of her pregnancy. They were both in bed for nearly a week. When the baby came, they named him William, and she saw it then, too. There was a weight to it. She heard it when the family and neighbors first uttered the name.

When spring came around, William sought to expand his plans for the land. As he planted, he collaborated with his neighbor Jim. They used new methods that people in Virginia spoke of, and raised more crops than they could have predicted. She could only imagine what ten years' time would produce on their plot.

But in this moment, as the rain came down on the strangers in the yard, all that had been stripped away. In ten minutes' time, he would likely be gone again. Howe was already a ghost, hiding in the corner of his house, armed but with no clear plan of escape.

"You've got to tell them that I ran off."

Hannah was frozen, trapped between rushing the children upstairs or holding them downstairs.

"Hannah, you need to tell them I ran. They're coming to the door—"

On cue there was a powerful knocking on the door. A silhouette crooked its head to attempt to peer in the window.

"Howe, let's go."

Hannah stared at the door, wanting to speak but unable to move. The baby began to squirm in his mother's rigid pose. The toddler hid between his father's knees, staring out from behind the rifle stock.

The door shook from another pounding. "Howe! It's Bitting. Augustus Bitting. I'm on the run like you. We've got to run. Bounty hunters are in the area. Now I'm not waiting long out here. We've got to get out now."

Howe spoke in a low whisper. "Isaac's nephew never said that name. Tell them I've gone." He held his son's hand and led him to his mother's side.

Hannah calmed herself through deep breathing. She squeezed the baby tight to her chest and wrenched the toddler close to her side. "William is not here!" A tremor of adrenaline shook through her. "He left. Early this morning."

She stared at the door, a window on either side with beaded raindrops glistening in the light of the single candle. Without moving, she heard the stairs behind her groan as William moved himself upstairs. In that moment she realized another change that had come over her husband since his time away. When he enlisted, she had doubted that he could ever kill another person. As the floorboards creaked above her head, she knew he was moving to the window.

"He's not here," she called again. "He's gone to Allentown."

The man on the other side of the door shed his performance. With a great pounding on the door, he hollered for her to open. "I know he is in there! I saw him this morning in town. He is under arrest for desertion. Now you open this door right now or you will both be taken under arrest!"

The beating on the door resumed as the shadow of a figure crossed the window moving toward the back of the house. Hannah stood as the baby began to cluck and whine against his mother's grip, and motioned to the toddler who went to the base of the stairs looking up for his father.

A flash of lightning lit the room, the deep rumble of thunder followed, and the baby's cry went off like a siren. At that, a sharp crack of a rifle shot rang out from the room above them, with secondary claps of shots responding outside in the yard.

Hannah was quick to the window where she could see silhouettes in motion. More shots popped outside as she gathered her children at the back of the room. The knocking of her husband's steps crossed the room above and descended the stairs behind her. The sharp cries of the baby filled the room, with the toddler's cries now joining in. As William took the baby, Hannah went back to the window. Another flash of lightning revealed a seated figure with two others tending to it.

"I shot first to scare them off—I didn't want them getting to you and the kids."

Hannah kept her focus on the men outside. "Did you kill him?"

"I didn't shoot him. They separated and thought I was running."

The baby gnawed on his father's thumb, and in the absence of the wailing they could hear that the rain had picked up. It drummed on the roof and windows, merging with a distant rumble of thunder.

"Bill, what happens now?"

As she watched the figures in the yard, she could see that the seated person was now laying flat. The other two crouched beside him with their heads down.

Her husband carried the baby to the dinner table. He laid his rifle across it and sat rolling the single discharged casing in his fingers. Out of reflex, Hannah joined him at the table with the toddler in tow.

"Listen. I shot once to scare them off. This here is the casing."

"Bill, what are we going to do?"

Herein she saw the greatest change in her husband. He was taking charge of a situation that he had no hopes to control. He was instilling confidence in her despite the fact that his had been emptied out.

"They're not going to leave—especially now. Take this casing. It was the only shot I fired. It won't match the round in him."

"How do you know that, Bill?"

"I shot a rifle, they've got pistols."

"Well, what am I going to do with it?"

"They'll search me and take it. You keep it. Give it to your father. That there is proof that I'm innocent. I only shot to scare them off. One shot. With that I'll be able to make my way back."

"Back from where?"

"Hannah, they're going to take me tonight."

The candle on the table before them had burned down to a feeble light. William wrapped his arms around both his sons and held them close in his lap. Hannah was rigid with disbelief. Through the drumming of the rain, they heard a slight knocking on the door. Almost casual.

William passed the baby to Hannah and gave Charles a focused hug, rocking him and whispering into his ear. "It'll be just like before. I'll be gone a bit and then come home safe and sound, quicker than you'll remember." He stood up. "We've plenty of stores this time around. Jim can help you with the rest." He placed the spent round on its end on the table in front of Hannah and called to the door. "I am coming out! I mean no harm!"

"Bill, you can't just leave like that. You served your time—you haven't been paid. They can't just arrest you. It's been six months. The war's nearly over—"

"Hannah, they're going to take me tonight. You keep that casing. I'll write to you when they take me wherever they take me. Probably to the prison in Philadelphia. I'm not going back to that war." He paused. "I'll have food and water, I'll state my case, and then I'll be free to come home."

Hannah remained sitting as he hugged her. He crossed the room and took a second candle to rob the flame from the first and replace it. Before opening the door, he took a deep breath and unlocked it.

Swinging the door open, William held his hands up as he was pulled out into the darkness of the storm.

10

John Brown's Tavern

There was a shuffling of bootsteps, the porch floorboards creaked. A sharp knocking on the door sounded.

Salter opened the door, which meant he was now open for business. He leaned on the door frame and squinted into the early afternoon sunlight. He scratched at the white hairs on his chin like a dog. "Howdy-howdy, boys. What can I help you with?"

At the onset of spring in 1864, a group of soldiers received orders to dig into the side of a hill and construct a small shed using large hardwood timbers. Off the side of the shed, standing proud of the sloping soil line, they mortared together a primitive chimney using fieldstones. With the building standing on its own in an earthen pocket, they doubled up the timbers along the walls, making them nearly four feet thick. Once firmly seated in the hillside, they laid the timbers on the roof and returned the hillside to its natural grade. The down-sloping brim above the entrance would be lined with sandbags and smaller timbers packed together with mud. After a few days' toil and the strained back of a mule, there sat a shelter they felt confident in declaring "bomb proof." It was where the men of higher rank would meet to choreograph their next step along the high-tide line of the Southern advance.

Satisfied with their efforts in architecture and uncomfortable with an extended lull in fighting, the men began construction of their own about two weeks later. On a small knob about a mile equidistant from the officer's shed and the rail line, they built and buried a shelter all their own, just as sturdy as the last, and nailed a board above the door that read *John Brown's Tavern*. Salter moved in and ran it as a sort of mercantile, selling or trading everything from shoe leather to satchels, doing his best to keep the soldiers in various states of readiness as they amassed before crossing the Mason-Dixon line.

After construction, with so many soldiers marching through farm country toward constricting battle lines, Salter found it best to sleep there and tend the shop around the clock. It was a sort of privilege of safety, and it was respected by the men who found comfort in the haberdashery being there.

With nearly all the trees around it felled for tent posts and firewood, *John Brown's Tavern* basked in the sun. Three young men stood on the porch, filthy and smelling like dogs. As Salter emerged from the dark interior, one of the soldiers asked, "Salter, you got a deck of cards in here?" He was a frail young man, covered in a thick film of sweat and dirt. His face had soft features and a tangled brown mane, with dark eye sockets and blood shot eyes that made him look like he hadn't slept since he enlisted. He held his hat in his hands standing on the porch, his companions standing just off the porch.

Salter looked the boys over. "I do, boys. I do," he said. "Only thing is they're missing the jokers."

One of the boys took a seat on the edge of porch. "Looks like twos will be wild." He rolled a cigarette.

Salter went to the dark back wall of the tavern, where it was lined with rough-cut shelving displaying battered and used goods from the floor to the ceiling. Along the dirt floor were fruit crates containing a sparse variety of items recovered from the deceased at battlefields farther west and south. He grabbed a deck of cards, removed the twine that held them, and fanned them out in his hand. His wiry white beard bobbed as he counted under his breath on his way to the porch.

"Here you are, boys. Suits are eagles, shields, stars,

JOHN BROWN'S TAVERN

and flags. We'll call it a nickel."

The soldier with the bloodshot eyes produced a coin from his pocket and flipped it in the air to Salter. Now both his companions had taken a seat on the lip of the porch, semi-reclining in the angle of the sun.

He said, "Thanks a nickel, Salter. Nice suits on these."

Salter grinned. "Don't matter the suit. Matters that you get an honest shuffle."

"You got quick hands, old man? I'll keep an eye on you." The boy's company chuckled.

"Oh, you don't have to be quick with the shuffle. Just have to look like you mean it while your mind's elsewhere."

A series of yips and hollering drew their attention to the encampment. A mandolin player was serenading a group of soldiers with *Richmond Is a Hard Road to Travel*. One of the soldiers sitting along the porch placed his cigarette in his mouth, his foot tapping along. The other shook his head as he carved a pipe from a piece of maple.

Beyond the musician, tents stood enveloped in the smoke of afternoon cook fires, and through the haze, lines of men marched and drilled to raps on a snare drum. The hillsides opened to a soft valley that spread itself wider to accommodate so many men at one time. Summer was settling into the countryside, lifting the dulled spirits of the men.

"All right, swindler," the soldier said. "How much for a sip?"

"Oh, now boys, the rest of the whiskey is to be sent to the field doctors. I wouldn't feel right having you drinking this early, anyway. Here, have a bit of coffee instead."

Salter stepped into his hut and returned with a small can. He held it to the boys, shaking the grains inside.

The soldier balked. The dark hoods of his eyes narrowed. "The field doctors?"

One of his seated companions added, "Well, we'll deliver it for you."

"In due time," Salter said. "When the next dance starts, I'll open the whiskey. That I can promise you." He placed the coffee tin on a barrel by the door. "We'll need it more than want it then."

"There is no 'we,' old man." The red-eyed soldier grabbed the can of coffee off the barrel.

Salter straightened his thin frame in the doorway.

"Get us the whiskey."

"Take the coffee, instead. That's what I have to offer."

"I don't give a goddamn what you're offering."

"Mind you! Have some respect."

"Respect—you're peddling the wares off of dead men. Hell, you'll probably sell these cards two or three more times!"

One of the reclining soldiers returned to his feet, dusting himself off. "I don't know. I've not had a coffee for days. Be almost like home."

The third still leaned his back against the porch post, squinting under the brim of his hat as he looked over the encampment.

Salter folded his arms, leaned against the door frame, and smiled. "Where you from, boy? Further north?"

"New York. Near the canal. These boys here are from western Pennsy."

"Well, I hope that those cards never change hands again. I do. But what little whiskey I have is for the doctors' use. Can't hardly waste a drop before the fighting."

"Come on, old man. I got a toothache. Just enough to wash my mouth out. Not a drop more."

"I'd rather not, son. Heat up the coffee and you'll feel soothed, I'm sure."

"Aw, you know what? To hell with you, Salter. We're serving the Union. You should respect us enough to sell us some goddamn whiskey. I ain't asking it as a favor."

The third boy was now on his feet. The soldiers stood shoulder to shoulder, six eyes on Salter. The expressions on their faces were as worn out as their uniforms.

Salter stood back in the doorway.

"I'm serving the Union, too, boy. The whiskey isn't for sale. It's medical supply."

"Don't kid yourself, old man. You're serving the devil. You're a glorified grave robber. If you wanted to serve, then you'd put on a uniform. Sure, you could steal one easy enough. Go and loot bodies and take everything but the coat."

His eyes were bright blue and pitiful under a web of red, shining out from his browned and weather-beaten face. The other two remained quiet. The boy distributed his weight onto both feet, crossed his arms, and spit. "Coward."

Salter glanced to the other end of the encampment where a barn was marked with a green "H" on a yellow field. A well-beaten path rippled out around the building, worn to dust by men shuffling about in a hurry, horses charging in with wagons from the battlefields, toting the limp weight of quiet soldiers. Beneath an overhang, limbs were piled loose like kindling in a wheelbarrow. A man walked briskly toward a well pump carrying a handsaw, his sleeves rolled up and his head down.

Salter's gaze fell to where the soldier had spit. His face reddened as the moment settled in. He inhaled as he shook his head.

"Please don't speak to me that way, boy."

"No, you watch how you speak to me, Salter. You're a goddamn parasite."

"You listen to me, you ungrateful son of a bitch. Where'd you be without me?"

"Salter, look around. Where'd you be without us? Baling hay?"

"I'm keeping you all from cannibalizing each other's belongings. Then the shame would be on you. But it's not. It's on me." He paused and drew his mouth into a long, thin line. His eyes were wide and focused.

The boys began to lose interest.

"That's my service," Salter said. "You listen to me. That's my service."

The red-eyed soldier slammed another nickel on the barrel and shook the can of coffee at Salter. The boys traded glances and began to turn away.

"If I'm going to live here so that you can play cards and sleep easy before the next march, and wake up to some goddamn coffee, then, yes, I'll be the one who makes the rules. Now don't you come back for no goddamn whiskey."

The boys were already making their way down along the old farming trails that were trampled into dirt roads. Without looking back, one raised the deck of cards over his shoulder. The roads bent and curved through the rolling hills, connecting scattered homesteads and farms, ringing in the rising crop of weathered canvas tents. North by northeast clouds of thick gray musket smoke veiled the high June sun and sank into the tree line where the farm fields ended and a forested stretch of land began.

Salter watched from the porch as the boys trod the red dirt road, their skin sun burnt, the golden buckles on their uniforms still glistening. Above their shoulders, cresting a hill about a mile out, was a silhouetted wagon train making its way east toward their encampment.

Salter was quick to his bunk, where a fold of bills was hidden underneath his chamber pot. He donned a coat and hat and was out the door and down the road in the hopes of replenishing his inventory.

A stocky man in Union Blues led the wagon train, his open wagon drawn by a fine white horse. He looked worn and terribly sweaty. Behind him were three more wagons. Two drawn by soldiers in uniform with horses rusty and black in color, and the last, a smaller enclosed wagon, drawn by a frail-looking man and a single mule, so dirty gray it was nearly yellow.

Salter approached with caution, waving his hat and stretching a grin. "Where you on your way to, friend?"

"Philadelphia," said the stocky man, "Fort Mifflin."

He never halted his horses, only pulled up on the reins, slowing to a pace that Salter could walk beside. The rest of his caravan slowed in step.

"Got any supplies in this train? The boys in this camp are awfully low on some basics. Been eating nothing but hard bread for a week."

"Might be nearing time for you to make a trip to Philadelphia yourself."

"Now, sir, I'm asking because the boys here are struggling. I'm not asking to be a bother. I'll pay a high price, considering the convenience. The time you get to Philadelphia, you'll end up with nearly twice the materials you got right now."

The stocky man pulled hard on the reins and shouted back to the wagoner behind him, who in turn echoed it back, and in a series of barks and jangling chains Salter had an audience.

"We've been on the road since last night. Haven't so much as stopped to piss. Can you set up a wash station and get us something fresh to eat?"

Salter was almost giddy. "Glory, hallelujah! Give me about a half an hour. You can park your wagons in that field above the shelter over there," he said, pointing to the makeshift tavern. "Let the horses get a bite. I'll throw some fresh water in the trough, too."

"Your name?"

"They call me Salter. I run a sort of market out of that shelter in the hill. Been here for the better part of a year. Haven't stocked up on supplies in some time."

The stocky man dismounted his wagon.

"Salter," he said. "I'm Mike Wagner. Now, we do have some canned goods and some recovered supplies on hand to sell, but our priority is getting a bite to eat and resting a spell. We've got to be on our way by midafternoon when the heat dies down. We're moving a damned deserter."

"That's all well and good, Mr. Wagner. We'll have you on your way by midafternoon, then."

Wagner talked to the other riders, and all promptly mounted their wagons and rounded them into the field atop the hill.

A thunder picked up in the distance to the south. A scattering of deer broke from the wooded lot, flushed from the other side. The tents began to rustle with activity. Two scouts on horseback emerged from the trees, shouting. The buglers began rallying the battalion. Men from the long tents called out orders, soldiers were on their feet and marching, and all the while the thunder of muzzle blasts rolled in from the horizon beneath the sharp raps of snare drums.

Salter stood along the road and watched the surge of duty among the tents. He saw men he knew and hardly knew take up arms, and he looked to the boys' empty tents and cookfire where the deck of cards and the coffee tin rested on a wooden crate.

Wagner and his men were dismounting their wagons under a large sycamore that stood sentinel atop the hill that *John Brown's* was burrowed into. The shot reports were muted and blended by distance with distinct pops jumping from the forested stretch. Salter turned toward the hillside, calling up to Wagner.

"Mr. Wagner! They're rallying the battalion. What the hell are you doing?"

Two of his men had dismounted their wagon, tied up their horses, and sat on the ground beneath the tree. The man with the mule was tending to something in the back of his enclosed wagon. Wagner put his hands on his hips, standing in silhouette.

"Not a concern of ours, Salter. You ready that bite just like you said you would."

The deep cannon blasts rattled in Salter's chest as he stepped up onto the tavern's porch. Muzzles flashed like fireflies in the haze of smoke and heat. With a chorus of shouts one line advanced on another, the cackling Rebel Yell rising in a shrill. Some of the Union soldiers were

John Brown's Tavern

pushed back through the row of trees, into the encampment. A battery of cannon fire cut a swath through the undergrowth. The invisible tug of a stray cannonball rolled up some tents on the periphery.

The fog of gun smoke rolled into the fields like weather. Salter looked up the hill to see Wagner and his men fully dismounted and conversing, pointing and making mute comments that couldn't carry over the racket in the fields. Salter stepped from the porch and hollered to Wagner again.

"Mr. Wagner, they're marching—," he called through deep breaths, "they're marching awfully close." Toward the last wagon Salter could make out a face that was pressed between two bars, looking out over the battle.

Wagner and his men walked down to where Salter was, looking just beyond him to the fighting farther below. It roared like a fire now, with musket fire crackling and strong smoke clouding the whole of the valley. The Rebel yells cut again through the cacophony.

"Our duty is transporting this here deserter—can't get involved in any fighting. Now, we'll see how this plays out. But when it does die down, my men'd appreciate some fresh food and water if it's still available."

"No, sir. You need to load these wagons with soldiers or supplies, ride them clear up to the line."

"Old man, I know you're hoping for a miracle but it ain't mine to provide."

"It ain't a miracle. It's duty."

"Please don't try to give me orders. You got your station, and we got ours. Our job is transporting these wagons and that deserter to Mifflin."

All five stood looking over as the thick smoke hung in valley, electric with staccato gunfire. "The more men that die, the better your business, anyway. That's why you aren't taking up arms and charging that clearing yourself."

The fighting began to dissipate as quickly as it had been sparked. Wagner glanced at one of the riders and nodded, then said to Salter, "Dying down now."

The soldiers began to emerge from the tree line, climbing through the brush without formation. They returned to their tents within the camp.

Salter watched the men outside of the medical barn as they stood looking on. A figure watched and waited on a horse hitched to an empty wagon. Salter said, "Sure enough, Mr. Wagner. Head over to that shelter there. I'll fix you something to eat, get you on your way."

Inside of the tavern, the men set up around a table. Salter lifted a crate from a stack to the floor and replaced its position with another, shuffling the goods about.

"I've got eight eggs here and some salt pork," he said. "Let me stoke the burner. I'll get this going on the skillet and grab some water to boil clean. Get some coffee going, too, gentlemen."

As Salter stepped out for an armful of split wood, he saw the tide of men continue to drift back in. There was still the soft clap of a distant report sounding here and there. The smoke was lifting, and the hillsides began to brighten in the distance.

Looking just beyond the tavern, he saw two of the boys returning to their tent where the deck of cards still sat on the powder keg table. As he approached them, they were recounting the choreography of the march.

Their narratives receded into an awkward silence. "You boys all right?"

"Sure, Salter," one of the boys responded. "Just tired." He sounded hollowed out.

"What happened out there? We moving camp?" Salter could see the boy reliving what he'd just survived.

"No. No need to move. It was a small battalion trying to set up on those western hills. We flushed them out. Hit hard by their reinforcements. Only lost a few men where they broke the line."

Salter nodded his head as the boy's partner sat down in silence.

John Brown's Tavern

"Where's the tall boy? The one who bought the cards?"

The soldier looked out to where the men were emerging from the woods. His eyes opened up like a break in the clouds. "He was at the break, Salter."

His partner sat on a cut stump, never looking up from the ground, his fingers folded around the barrel with the stock between his feet. Salter stared to the west, where the gun smoke merged with the rising clouds to form an empyrean wall at the end of the encampment.

The silent boy spoke from beneath a downturned brim. "Don't touch those goddamn cards, old man."

His old legs carried him past the stack of split wood between trees next to the tavern. He stomped inside, Wagner's men all turning toward his motion. He had grabbed a crate that was covered by a gray wool blanket and set it on the table next to Wagner. Removing the blanket, he revealed two bottles of whiskey and several loaves of dried bread.

"Now help yourselves, boys. I'll cook the pork and eggs outside on the open pit. You take a load off. Just got a report that the fighting's likely over for the day."

Wagner grabbed four tin cups from a shelf and dealt them. He grunted through his nose and bobbed his head.

Salter faked a grin, removed his hat with one hand and rustled his white hair with the other. "Just be another minute 'til the fire's on."

He walked back into the sun-beaten landscape where he saw the two boys sitting outside their tents, one cleaning out the barrel of his musket, the other still hanging his head. Salter hurried over and without a word, approached one of the boys and forced the flask of whiskey into his hands. He said only, "Medicine."

Notes from a Deserter

In the field behind *John Brown's*, Salter emptied a few crates from the smallest of Wagner's wagons and placed them at the base of the tree. All that was left in the wagon were some blankets, the man's satchel with a single shot pistol, a few baskets, and a shovel. As he organized the goods, he heard a low voice from the larger wagon. "There's a shotgun on the seat of this wagon."

"I ain't breaking you out."

"I ain't aiming to break out. I fought. Not like old Wagner." His voice had a wooden echo from within the carriage cell.

"Who the hell are you to judge?"

"If Wagner could kill someone himself, I wouldn't be in this wagon."

Salter stepped up to the seat of the enclosed wagon, and pulled the shotgun from where it was propped between the seat and rail. He walked up to the window and looked in at the deserter, sitting against the back wall with his knees drawn up and his hands flat on the floor. Three beams of sunlight draped over his sulking form.

Salter said, "What's your name?"

"William."

"How come you deserted?"

The prisoner tilted his head back against the wall and said, "I did everything they asked of me."

"Then why'd you run?"

"Thought I was dying. Awful sick. Fought sick. Couldn't lay freezing in a camp. No doctor would see me. All my officers dead or headed to Philadelphia."

Salter wrapped his hands around the bars of the window, pressing his face into the space between. "So, you fought?"

The man said only, "Fredericksburg."

Salter leaned away from the bars, checking for any onlookers. When his eyes refocused on the dark interior of the cell, the deserter had moved closer to the window.

"Salter, I need a favor."

John Brown's Tavern

"I told you, I ain't breaking you out. You chose your fate."

"I know." From his tattered clothes he produced two envelopes and slipped them between the bars. "Just these."

"Mail?"

"One's to Pennsylvania Avenue."

"You and old Honest Abe friendly—?"

"I'm just asking for a pardon. Stating my case."

Salter scanned his surroundings again. "And the other?"

"To my wife."

Salter scoffed. "There's no postage on these."

William returned to a seated position at the back of the cell. "Put it on Wagner's tab."

"What tab? I'm not sending these without—"

Salter could hear Wagner and his men laughing in the tavern. He slapped the envelopes across his thigh, and then peered into the wagon. "You know, might as well just throw these in the fire."

"I left my family to serve, now I've been taken from them again. Please. Send them."

Salter paused, resting his head against the rough wood of the wagon. A volley of muskey shots crackled off in the distance, followed by the deep thundering cannons. Wagner called for Salter.

He raised his head. "William—good luck, if you're pardoned."

Dust was suspended in focused beams of light that reached into the cell. William lifted his head, and the light fell on his face.

"Same to you, Salter."

Salter returned to the smaller wagon with a knapsack strapped on his back, untied the horse from a low limb, mounted the animal and rode to the foothills. The setting sun diffused the gun smoke into an afternoon haze.

Wagner stepped to the door as Salter crested the shoulder of the hillside surrounding the encampment about

119

a mile out. He scrambled up the hill to his supplies, but by the time he reached his rifle, Salter was out of range. "I'll be a son of a bitch," he said. Turning to his men he called, "Take whatever supplies you need for the ride. The old man just commandeered a goddamn wagon. All that's here is ours now."

He raised his rifle to fire a warning shot. Pressing it to his shoulder he found that Salter had taken the ammunition.

Crossing through the hedge line, Salter pulled back on the reigns and asked a few details of some of the last men to leave the battlefield along the red clay road. They had used the stone walls around an orchard as an abutment of cover against a small surge of Rebels. The men pointed him toward the initial point of contact between the two sides where the corner of the orchard was breached.

He tied the horse to a tree and retrieved his supplies from the wagon. Resting a shovel across his shoulder he proceeded on foot along a trodden dirt path. The black horse shook its head at the dangling reins. A small creek glistening in the sun beneath the smoke crossed the orchard at an angle. The clouds had risen high in the air, and the sun sank low beneath it.

Several men lay scattered in the field, coughing and gasping from wounds. A few survivors picked their way through the field, assessing which bodies would need transported and which would need buried there in the grassy field.

Salter made his way along the loosely stacked wall that separated the orchard from the heavy forest growth to a corner where the stream broke into a wooded lot in deeper shaded pools. In the shadow of the gray stone wall a deep blue form took shape. Long and thin, and soaked to a purple hue with blood, there lay the boy who bought the cards.

His face was agape and blood-spattered, a vacant stare lost in the patch of green that his body rested in. Salter stood a moment in disbelief. He looked back the way he came, the haze nearly lifted from the orchard, leaving it empty and stretching out in a diamond shape.

He sat on the wall beside the boy's body, removed his hat, and placed it on the crown of his bent knee. A shovel rested against his shoulder. He pressed his elbow on his knee, the palm of his hand supporting the weight of his head. Nightfall came early away from the expansive clearing of the farm fields. The evening glow settled in under a full moon, stretching the sky tight and dark. The fireflies floated in earthen constellations. Salter began to dig.

Humming as he worked, he would break when he became tired and coated in a layer of soil. He kneeled by the small stream and washed his hands half-heartedly. His sleeves were rolled and laden with dirt, the cuffs coughing dust with the shaking motion of his arms. The earth beneath the topsoil had been soft and moist, leaving the knees of his pants caked with a fine layer that felt wet against his thighs.

The wooden shovel was rough and weathered, blistering his hands. His work soon yielded a shallow grave. He rested on the lip of the hole, then laid back into the dew of the grass. He felt tired and old.

He rinsed his hands once more in the stream and dampened a cloth which he used to clean the fallen soldier's face. He dragged the body a few feet to the grave and began to cover the boy over.

Returning to the stone wall, he reached into his knapsack and pulled out a small, tattered flag, wrapped a stone in it, and placed it on the resting mound of dirt. Salter had lined everything that belonged to the boy along the top of the wall. A pocketknife was etched with his initials. The overcoat had been punched through by a bullet and soaked with blood. A small satchel of black powder was tied up with a simple knot. The musket was tarnished and scratched.

Notes from a Deserter

    Salter donned the boy's repaired blue vest, stiffened with patches of blood. The Union cap was still sweated at the brim as Salter positioned it on his head. He left the shovel lying there and took up the boy's musket.

11

A Flimsy Gallows

Two men approached a pile of building supplies that were gathered in the yard. One man stood sweating through a yellowed civilian shirt, suspenders lifting his light blue woolen trousers. He wore a primitive farmer's hat, thin hide pressed into a tall, almost conical shape, with a brim that hung low and blocked the sun. Shrouding his eyes, it made his wide grin pronounced.

The other unbuttoned his deep blue Union overcoat, the tiny brim of his forage cap offering little protection from the midday sun. His eyes were nearly closed as he looked at the younger man before the pile of supplies. "Morning, Henry."

Henry removed the floppy hat and held it out from his hip with his elbow crooked, placing one foot on the pile of wood, rubbing the top of his thigh. He took a deep breath in through his nose and exhaled through a puckered smile. The heat was bottled up by the walls of Fort Mifflin.

"Matthew, how we doing today?"

"Not so bad, young man. Not so bad." He perused the pile of supplies. "Any nails to go with this timber? I'm no Amish carpenter."

"That crate over there. Nails and hammers." He arched his back and located the sun. "I drew up some plans this morning."

Henry handed a small piece of paper to Matthew. It was roughly drawn, and though Matthew hadn't a clue whether the structure depicted would stand sturdy, he asked a few clarifying questions about the illustration, adding, "I haven't built much since I left my father's farm. Christ, that was nearly twenty years ago."

"Not much of a carpenter myself," said Henry, counting back five years to when he left his family's homestead.

"Makes you wonder why we're on gallows duty."

"It'll stand. He weighs less than 200 pounds. And he needn't hang for long if he falls a good bit. That alone should break his neck."

Matthew lifted his hat, ran his hand over the tangled mess of graying hair, and replaced his hat. "Who else is giving us a hand with this?"

Henry's masked grin grew. "They're resetting the battery. Most everyone'll be outside the walls for the day. Well, until tonight, of course."

"You believe they sold tickets for it?" Matthew exhaled a soft decrescendo of aitches, shaking his head. "Poor bastard."

Henry smacked his hat against his legs, freeing dust from both his trousers and the hat. He crouched with wide knees beside the supplies, elbows on thighs and both hands turning his hat by the brim. Never looking up he said, "Why not just execute him, if he really committed such a wrong?"

Matthew stepped to his left, draping his shadow over Henry. "That's what we're going to do. Execute him."

"Well, we're not really executing him."

"Not you and me, no."

"No, I mean the hanging. Why bother with all of this? Why not just shoot him?" Henry looked up at Matthew, one eye shut, one eye squinting.

"Well, who would shoot him?"

"Whoever says he's guilty." He stood up, ran his hand through his hair and returned his hat to his head with a sweeping motion. "Whoever says he's guilty is the executioner, somebody else just does the dirty work."

Matthew began taking off his coat. "Are we doing the dirty work?"

"I haven't seen the judge all day. Must mean it's us."

Chuckling and rolling his sleeves, Matthew took note that Henry had hardly worn the Union uniform. "Where's your hat and coat?" he said.

"Hat's in on my bunk. Prefer my own issue. And that damn coat is awful warm for dirty work."

The two began separating the timbers by diameter, placing the thicker lengths in a pile to use for the building of the base. The thinner branches and planks would be used as a rugged decking for the platform.

"No shovel." Henry stood before the sorted poles. "I'll get a shovel. Must be one in the guard house."

"Can't go in the guardhouse. Don't need a shovel." Matthew wiped the sweat from the sides of his face, looked at his wet fingers, and then wiped again. "Main post will have to be attached to the frame."

"No. Then the frame'll need to be heavier all the way around. I'd rather dig for ten minutes apiece and do it right. No sense spending more time on the framing."

He started walking toward the guardhouse on the other side of the yard, the heat of the day pressing on the open space.

"Henry, go get it out of the stable outside the wall. They won't let you in that guardhouse."

He stopped and turned, breathing through bared teeth. "Why not?"

"They're keeping the accused in there. Howe. He's in that back room right there."

Henry turned back to the guardhouse; a small one-story brick building, twice as long as it was tall, with a chimney at the far end. There were three windows, all with vertical bars. The third and final window had two pale hands wrapped around the bars. They slowly released and faded into the blackened square. Henry stood for a moment with his head down. The warm sun on his back tilted his shadow in the direction of the cell. He turned and marched out to the stable.

Returning with the shovel, he walked past Matthew

without a word, stepped beyond the arrangement of poles lying flat on the ground, and began to dig. He kept his face down, the sweat gathering at the tip of his nose before dropping to the dry soil.

"He's a risk," Matthew said. "Had to keep him under watchful eye."

"Well, who's watching who? He can probably hear every word we're saying." Henry stepped hard into the back end of the spade.

"Lincoln himself could let him go. Howe supposedly wrote to him twice. That's a judge *and* the president who say he's guilty. All we've got to do is follow orders."

"Funny, didn't see either when I went for the shovel."

Matthew held out his hand and shooed Henry. "You said it yourself. Dirty work." He took the shovel and began digging the hole wider.

Henry went to the largest post, what would be their center post, and rolled the end to the lip of the hole. He straddled it and sat, watching Matthew sweat and dig. He spoke in a whisper now, his eyes peering from the shade of his brim to the white wall of the guardhouse. "You know why he deserted them boys down south?"

Matthew stood up straight, attempting to touch his elbows behind his back. He stepped to Henry, shovel handle first, lowered his voice and said, "Yea, he was down at the battle of Fredericksburg." Henry took the shovel handle, and they replaced positions. Matthew sat on the log, still speaking in a soft, polite tone. "Put the scare in him. A month later he turned up missing. Went back up to Pennsylvania."

"He had dysentery, though. They say he lost twenty-five pounds. What good was he to the Union?" Henry drove the shovel.

"There were some men in worse shape than him who stayed and fought."

"Some men died just the same. You know as well as I do, more men die sick than shot at."

A Flimsy Gallows

"You can't know such a thing."

Henry reached the shovel into the hole to check the depth. "If you had dysentery, would you be building a platform right now?"

Matthew only turned and looked to the last window on the guardhouse.

"How far down should I go?" Henry was coated in a film of perspiration and grit. His clothes were sopped close to his body.

"Until it makes sense."

"Well, how far makes sense?"

"This pole's about fourteen, sixteen foot, or so. I'd say a good three to four feet. Then we can brace it low. Little further. You wanted to dig, boy."

The sun peaked, casting light to the bottom of the post hole. The men had no shadows but were outlined in dark lines by their saturated clothing. There was hardly any wind within the walls, and every little sound carried through the yard. Both men worked in silence, listening to the staccato echoes that were pinched in between the wall and the guardhouse with every shovel load. Old Glory flapped in muffled claps, catching gusts of wind high above the parched grounds.

Matthew produced two canteens from a satchel by the timbers. He reached one to Henry before helping himself. He watched Henry drink. "You know, he's not being hung just for deserting. He killed the soldier who tried to arrest him."

"Not according to him—way he tells it to folks is the bounty hunters were drunk. He fired to scare them off, but never shot to kill."

"Oh, heavens. What else would he say?"

Henry squatted beside the hole, sliding the shovel in to check the depth again. "How's that?"

Matthew spoke deliberately. "If you take a prisoner's word, they're all innocent."

"All I'm saying—"

"All I'm saying is it's nonsense. You listen."

He stepped round the edge of the hole and crouched beside Henry. He lowered his voice to a whisper once more. "They find this little stone house up in the hills there outside of Philadelphia. The soldiers knock and knock and knock. Finally, his wife comes to the door—he sent his wife to the door!"

"Matthew, I—"

"Hold on now, this is the part you're asking for." He looked over his shoulder at the guardhouse, then looked down at the hole and chuckled. "His old lady says he's not home. Calls out the window, 'No, sir. William's not here. Never made it back from the war.' Some song she was singing. Anyway, to make a long story short, they kicked in the door and he's there hiding with his kids. They try to arrest him. The bastard gets loose and leads them back out into the yard. He puts a bullet in the belly of one of the officers. He's lucky they—"

"Matthew, I meant how's that for depth?"

"Oh. It's good. That's a good depth."

Matthew took a seat on the end of the timber post and wiped the sweat from the back of his neck.

Henry stood up. "Where were you when all that went on?"

"When what went on?"

"The arrest. You make it sound like you were tying up their horses."

"No. Not at all. I was here, likely. What's that got to do with anything?"

"Sounds like awful far for you to have a clear vantage. Hell, we're at sea level here."

Henry grabbed a rope and tossed it at Matthew. "Tie that up there where the pole is notched. We'll hoist it in, then set it with some gravel from the road and a dirt-and-water mix."

Matthew walked to the far end of the post. He tied it off and pulled the rope taught from a few yards away. Lifting

A Flimsy Gallows

the thin end of the post up, Henry walked his hands down the timber as Matthew pulled the rope. The timber slid to the edge of the hole, sank through the rim and toppled in. Henry hugged it close as Matthew walked shovel loads of gravel from the path to the hole. Soon it was sturdy enough to stand on its own, and Henry made quick work of braces to keep it from teetering to one side or the other. While affixing the brace low, he said, "Can I ask you something, Matthew?"

He nodded, spreading his legs to control the sway of the pole.

"You have kids?"

"I do. Three kids. Oldest is probably close to your age now."

"All right. Well, imagine you leave the service sick as a dog. You somehow find a way back home, with your kids, and look to get healthy. Two men come to your house and kick your door in. What would you have done?"

"I wouldn't have murdered someone."

"Well, what would you have done?"

Matthew looked up to the top of the post and exhaled, then looked down at Henry. He spoke with confidence, allowing his voice to carry in through the little guardhouse window. "Any man who motions to take the life of another is a murderer. And he ought to be hanged."

"But what would you have done?"

"Oh, Jesus Christ Henry. Why not go break him out then?"

"They didn't have to make him watch us build the gallows. He fought for the Union."

"Henry, just finish the goddamned brace."

"This is the closest to the fighting I've gotten so far. Building a damned gallows on Mud Island. He fought at Fredericksburg, against actual graybacks."

"Let go, see if it holds." Matthew nudged him away from the post.

The pole stood, turning the courtyard into a small

sundial that was counting down to the evening's execution.

"If a Rebel broke in tonight to this fort, what would you do?"

Matthew kneaded his forehead. He clenched his lips together and exhaled deeply through his nose. He spoke while nodding to himself, "I'd shoot the son of a bitch. I'd send his body back to the Carolinas."

"Why?" He picked up a saw to cut the platform posts to equal heights.

"Oh, come on, Henry."

"Howe is a threat, just the same. Based on accounts he's killed more Union soldiers than some of the more cowardly Rebels. Go shoot him."

"Stop with this." Matthew laughed to himself under the pressure and stepped in a half circle with his hands on his hips and his shaking head looking down into a shadow. "I ain't a murderer, Henry. I ain't no goddamn murderer."

Henry tossed the saw at Matthew's feet. "Neither am I."

In a fury, he grabbed a pry bar from the tool crate, and pried off the braces. In one easy push he felled the main post that rattled to the ground in loud echoes like gunfire. Matthew stood and watched as he threw the pry bar at the guardhouse. Never speaking, only grunting like a child subduing emotions, he lifted his hat, wiped his hair, replaced the hat, and took pause at the hands on the bars of the window. He made his way to the bunkhouse and disappeared into the dark entrance.

Matthew laughed to himself. "Youth," he said as he picked up the satchel, stood for a moment surveying the supplies, looked upward to the relentless sun, and headed to the outhouse where he might sort out the events of the afternoon. On his way past the guardhouse, an officer stepped from the doorway and bristled at the extreme heat.

"What the hell is going on out here, Matthew?"

In stride with his head down he said, "Henry boiled over. I think the heat got to him. Give him an hour or so.

A FLIMSY GALLOWS

We'll get it done when the heat dies down a little."

"Matthew, we don't have all the time in the world. They sold tickets for tonight."

He stopped and turned to the officer. "Well, if you're in a hurry you could just shoot him yourself."

"What the hell is that supposed to mean, Matthew?"

"Suppose it means that you'll wait."

He resumed his course to the latrines, leaving the courtyard empty of anything but a flag and a mirage.

※

When the heat of the day began to subside, Matthew crossed the courtyard. He stood over the building supplies as if viewing them for the first time. His shadow reached out in front of him, and as he rolled a post over with his foot, he lifted his eyes but not his head and looked to the window. In the blackened square, there may have been a face behind the bars.

He placed his satchel beside the supplies and tossed his hat on top. Cupping a brim with his hand he squinted to the bunkhouses, where he was no better at discerning the shapes through shadowed windows. He let out a loud alarming whistle, which bounced around the walls of the fort. The only thing that stirred was Howe's hands, which returned to the bars of the guardhouse window. A sweeping shadow of a bird circled the courtyard before spiraling to the outer walls. Matthew looked to the hands and tried to make out eyes based on proportion.

He kicked dust across the yard and was quick into Henry's bunkhouse. Inside it was dark and cool, and the transition left him sun-blind and blinking heavily. As the fog sharpened, he took note of six beds, five of which were made up with bedding. At the foot of the single open bed was a Union Blue coat and hat, clean and folded.

※

Outside the wall of the fort, Henry entered the stable

with a pack slung over his shoulder. The soldier who ran the stable was getting ready to lay down for a midafternoon nap where the overhang of the stable merged with the shade of a tall oak tree.

"I need to borrow a horse for about an hour," he said, grinning again from beneath the floppy brim of his primitive hat.

"Where you going with it?"

"We're a little light on supplies for the gallows. Need a small portion of nails. Won't take me long."

The soldier wore an air of skepticism. He took a bite from an apple, and chewing with his whole face, he pulled a knot tight on his makeshift hammock. "Is this thing going off tonight, or what?"

"The sooner I get back, the better. Not much of a hanging if the gallows' not been built."

The soldier sat into the hammock, tossed Henry the rest of his apple, and then laid back awkwardly. "Take one of the bay horses," he said, "and hurry back. They sold tickets for tonight. Guess everyone knows, there ain't nothing worse than a deserter."

12

Witnesses

"Mary, look how close that heron is. Too close."

"Oh, Margaret, we've seen herons before. Might as well be our state bird."

Margaret lifted her dress in preparation for escaping an attack. "I've never seen one so close. Look at those ugly, wide-open eyes," she said. "Has a simple look on its face. Awful neck. I'm liable to strangle that thing if it comes any closer."

"Now how could you say such a thing?" Mary dabbed the beading sweat on her neck with a folded white cloth. "It's a beautiful blue and white. If it had any cardinal red, it'd be a walking stars and stripes."

"Well, aren't you generous?"

"It is called a 'great blue' heron for a reason, Margaret."

Margaret took Mary by the arm, and they proceeded away from the large bird as it poked through the reeds along the bank.

"'Blue' would do the job just as well." Margaret chuckled. "I'll give it credit for its grace—something that's lacking over these years." She opened her fan and began sweeping it before her face. "Still, it's an awful sight up close. Just awful."

The heat pressed exasperated breaths out of the crowd that gathered before the walls of Fort Mifflin. Soldiers congregated in casual conversation as civilians arrived aboard a steam-tug. The two frail women stood between the dock and the main gate of the fort with their dark dresses absorbing sunlight. They looked out over the marshland and the broad waters of the Delaware River.

A guard called to them, though he seemed unmoved by the season or the event. He waved to the spectators without ever getting up from a hammock that was slung under a canopy extending from the stable.

Mary leaned into Margaret so that the brims of their hats overlapped, and she spoke through her teeth as they approached the entrance to the fort.

"When I was leaving the latrine over there, I heard a soldier talking to an officer. Said it was the hardest thing he ever had to witness... this boy parting with his family."

"Boy? What boy?"

"The boy they're going to hang."

A young man in an oversized uniform collected their tickets at the gate, and the women passed into the main courtyard of Fort Mifflin.

Mary continued, "The soldier sounded devastated. Wish'd he hadn't seen it."

"He's wearing the thought of it now. Just look at him. That must be him. Pale as a seagull up there."

Margaret bobbed her bonnet toward a soldier who set the platform of the gallows, took his position beside it, and pulled the release. The wooden trap door clapped open, echoing through the yard. All of the townspeople gathering outside of the walls turned their head toward the sound. The heron lifted itself into the air and glided a short distance away.

"Yes," Mary said. "That's him. That must be him."

In the heat, the figure moved about in a blur behind the radiating waves of the yard. He reset the platform, straightened his uniform, and marched off with his head down. A strong breeze blew in from the water, encouraging the stragglers outside of the walls to be herded inward.

Mary leaned in to finish her story. "'Matthew,' the officer says," she mimicked a deeper voice, "'you are serving your country. Carry yourself like a soldier and fulfill your duty.' He said it real rough-like."

Margaret shook her head. "Poor soul."

Soldiers crisscrossed the yard from one building to another. The soldier who was to be the executioner, Matthew, was standing alone in the shade of the barracks entryway, facing the building beside the gallows. He fixed his gaze on a single window at the end of the building, where the accused may have been staring back from the obscure, darkened, and barred square.

"They shouldn't have put that boy in that position," Mary said.

"Well, now, don't forget, Mary. The boy is a soldier. I imagine they ought to do a great many things they'd prefer not to."

"And I'd have preferred not to come at all. We've no business being here, Margaret."

"My son served in this uniform and if someone brought shame on it, well, I'd like to see him brought to justice. Be it this boy—this soldier or any other."

"What comes first? The boy or the soldier?"

"How do you mean?"

Mary dabbed her white cloth about her neck again. "Well, they grow up as boys and go off to be soldiers. What are they when they come back?"

"They're boys, just the same," Margaret answered in a dismissive tone, then went on to contradict herself. "Not boys—who's to say they're all one or the other? Folks in Virginia saw a dead Yank, I'm sure, but he was my boy through and through the whole time."

"He was a soldier to more people than he was a boy." Mary turned her eyes to the gallows for the first time, where the rope hung loose with the noose resting limp on the platform. "I'm worried they're hanging a boy today. But hanging a soldier might even be worse."

A man in uniform interrupted, "They're hanging a murderer today, ma'am. Rest easy on that."

He was a tall man with a thick brow ridge and an arm that ended in a cloth wrap just below the elbow. His blue cap was too small for his head and wasn't so much worn by the man as it was resting atop his head. The blue roots of his beard shaded high on his cheeks, as if it grew in as a thick layer of fur and had to be cut to be tamed.

He split the women. "Pardon, ladies. If you'd follow the group over there, we'd like to keep civilians from wandering the yard. They'll be starting shortly."

"Sure thing, dear," Margaret said.

"Another nice boy there."

"Oh, Mary. You think all these boys are nice just because they're soldiers?"

"Well, it says something about them, I think."

"Nice boys killing other nice boys?"

The wind blew in gusts off of the water again, and the civilians clasped their hats as they turned their backs toward the source. A crowd of about fifty now milled about the scaffolding of the gallows like livestock beside a windmill. The heron rode the wind over the fort and off to the west, its broad shadow sweeping the topography of the people in the yard.

"This way, ladies." The soldier sidled beside Margaret, placed his only hand on her back as he guided her through the yard. "You sound like you might have some questions about the condemned," he said. When he turned his face to the sun, his eyes appeared to recede into their shadowed sockets. He smiled as a counterbalance to his dark features.

"Well, what's he done?" Margaret fanned herself as Mary inspected their companion from the corner of her eye. "He deserted—run off home when there was fighting to be done?"

The soldier arched his furry brow. "You make it sound like such a little thing. This one, Howe, he deserted the army at Fredericksburg when the Union needed him most."

"Fredericksburg," Mary said. "Horrible loss for the Union, if I recall correctly. Scared him off, did it?"

"Well, to be honest, ma'am, they do say he fought honorably. Quite so, quite so. Did the Union a service for the time he stayed. I guess it was too much for him—afterward, that is." He swept his hand from left to right, adding, "Had enough."

The trio met the edge of the spectators in the lot and the soldier nodded to the women, motioning to leave. Margaret grabbed his arm and asked, "Well, if he served in such a way, then what's the difference?" Removing her hand and stepping back in line with Mary, she added, "Is that all he's done?"

"No, no, ma'am. That's not all he's done, but deserting isn't nothing. They hang men for that alone." The soldier raised his brow and voice. "He killed a Union soldier that caught him deserting. Shot him right in the belly. Not to mention the tunneling incident here—"

"Why'd he shoot him?" Margaret's tone was that of someone who knew the truth and was testing to see it recited accurately. Individuals in the crowd pivoted away from the scaffolding and towards the two women.

"Howe's an unusual type. He's nice enough. A clever guy. Was awfully quiet at times, and then other times he tried to break out and run like wild. Imbalanced fellow."

Mary was still monitoring Matthew, a man she didn't know but pitied. She repeated the soldier's words to herself. "Imbalanced fellow."

"Could be soldier's heart." He tipped the brim of his cap up. "I'd be lying if I said it didn't keep me up at night from time to time. Can't know a thing like that for sure, I guess." From across the yard an officer let out a whistle that was stifled by the wind. "If you'll excuse me, they're motioning for us to take our position."

As he circumvented the crowd the glistening faces followed him. He joined a row of soldiers facing the crowd beside the gallows. The quiet murmur of the spectators settled as Matthew approached, sweating through his Union Blues. He took his place beside the platform and stared out with a look of desperation worthy of the prisoner himself.

Mary's gaze was still fixed on Matthew. "He made it home and they came to steal him back. Is that dishonoring the uniform?"

Margaret did not answer. There was a murmur rolling through the crowd as the guardhouse door opened and several soldiers shifted in and out of the building.

Howe emerged from the glowing white building in the center of the yard with a complacent look. He wore the blue wool pants of his uniform with a plain, yellowed shirt rolled at the cuffs. Two soldiers led him in chains to the gallows and helped him up the steps to the platform.

"His wife still here, Mary?"

"I haven't a clue what she looks like."

"The story you heard, where he said goodbye to them—"

"Margaret, I haven't got a clue."

An onlooker turned to hush the women. "He's about to speak."

Matthew read the death warrant aloud. The wind carried off most of his stammering words before they reached the listeners in the yard. He paused midway through the document, stood for a moment gazing down at the page in silence, and then read the disclaimer through to its conclusion. When he finished, he did an about face and stood for a moment atop the platform steps before descending each step with the full weight of his body lurching from side to side. He continued behind the scaffolding and stood a good distance away from both the onlookers and the soldiers, drawing the gaze of his fellow soldiers and officers alike. He crossed his arms and dipped his head to veil his eyes.

Howe stepped forward on the platform with his accompanying guards flanking him on both sides. His faint voice tumbled out. It was difficult for those in attendance to hear if he spoke plainly or recited a prayer. The few times he lifted his head, he looked above those congregated before him, to the wall behind them.

Speaking in hot whispered breaths, Margaret continued her search. "Do you see his wife? She must be here?"

"Be here? She had to've left. She couldn't keep children here. It's not proper—"

"That's right—the children. But she could have come back alone."

"You drug me here," Mary said. She shrugged, unfolded her cloth, and used the full length to wipe her brow to her neck before folding it and tucking it away. "Shame on the uniform and all the rest."

"That woman there. Do you think that's her?"

Through the crowd of heads Margaret spotted a young woman in a dark gown, her bonnet hiding her face. Her head was down, her shoulders slouched. As Margaret watched her, she inhaled and turned her face skyward. Her bonnet still hid her face, but she could see her shift the weight of a baby from one hip to the other. Margaret couldn't see the baby, either. Only the telltale bobbing and swaying one does to settle a newborn.

Margaret propped herself up on the tips of her toes to see if more children were beside her, pressing on Mary's shoulder to balance. "Mary, I think that is her. Must be."

"You've lost your mind. That woman is the same age as me. That black bonnet is probably older than the boy they're hanging."

Another adamant hush from those standing around them silenced the women, but Margaret still craned her neck and scanned each female face in the crowd.

"No, not that black one. It's more of a dark blue. Can't hardly see her face."

Mary took Margaret by the arm and pulled her into a hunch. Speaking into her ear, she said, "I can't hear a word this poor boy is saying. See if you can hear."

The few times his voice rose above a mumble it was lost beneath the flap of the flag in the yard and the laughing gulls that rode the spiraling wind currents above. He stopped to gather himself several times; a great breath would inflate his body only to leak out, leaving him hunched over more with each breath. He was dying before the crowd.

The only person he made eye contact with was the reporter, near to the front of the crowd, who was scribbling at furious pace trying to mark every word.

"Can't hear at all in this blasted wind," Margaret agreed. "What all is he saying?"

The man in front of them turned and spoke in short, sharp bursts. "Won't confess to what he did, the dog. Sob story about his family. Asked God for forgiveness—please now."

"His wife must be broken to hear his finals," Margaret mumbled to herself, dipping her head.

The man turned shaking his head. Mary leaned into Margaret and said, "You let that woman alone."

"You saw the one I was talking about? The dark blue bonnet?" Margaret's eyes opened wide to scan the crowd. "Guess it was black, but new-black. Deep color."

When he had finished, Howe nodded to the reporter, who nodded back. The officers and soldiers at the base of the scaffolding converged in an animated discussion. Matthew never did take his position with the other soldiers. He sat, instead, in the slight angle of shade the wall provided to the south of the spectators. His head curled down onto his raised knees, motionless.

It was the soldier who escorted the women to their spot that was coaxed to approach the lever at the base of the scaffold. Two soldiers on the platform above fitted Howe with a black hood. They adjusted the rope, one patting Howe on the back as if to wish him good luck, and they dismounted the platform. The dark-faced soldier shook his head as he took the release in his only hand.

Mary mumbled a phrase into her shawl. She turned and marched with hurried steps out of the gate, the white cloth flapping in as she went.

At her start, the soldier on the trigger glanced up. He recognized that now all eyes were on him, and the weight

WITNESSES

of his duty brought his hand and the release down. The platform let out a muffled clap as Howe's hooded head was drawn skyward.

The woman that Margaret had chosen didn't so much as flinch. She might as well have been looking beyond the scaffolding to the gulls that drifted down and crashed into the water. The witnesses in the yard were drawn into such a silence that Margaret could hear the rope straining under the victim's weight. She turned at last to see his last few panicked kicks, as if he were being lowered into a fire.

The breeze came in off of the water, forcing many in the crowd to put a hand atop their heads and turn their shoulders and backs into the wind. Standing so, it gave them an astonished look. Margaret's hat was lifted off and went rolling along unpursued. The rigid body was lifted slightly into the air toward the crowd against the taught rope. It hung there for a moment until the wind died down and the body swung like a pendulum, toward and then away from the onlookers. The scaffolding shrugged forward and backward under the dead weight of the hooded body.

There was no sound from the crowd strong enough to carry through the wind. Margaret watched as the soldier who pulled the release reached out to stop the body from swaying, using the stub of his arm and his free hand to settle the motion. Some men in uniform saluted the flag as it whipped its folds in the wind. All persons, living and dead, were stilled under the August sun.

Margaret studied the ground beneath her with wide, unfocused eyes as she exited the gate. She joined Mary outside of the wall. Without speaking, they walked arm in arm to the corral, where they mounted a wagon and waited for a stable hand to take them back to the city.

The sky was a featureless blue. Wind rushed up behind the women, pressing them along the road. The bright wall around the fort reflected and amplified the sun, while the river scattered the light along its flashing surface. And from behind the wall, the black silhouette

141

of the gallows reached like a flagpole without a banner. Margaret averted her gaze, searching for the heron in the reeds through glassy eyes.

    A driver mounted the wagon and with a short word readied the horses. After inspecting the harness and reins, he took his seat at the front of the wagon. He removed a cloth from his pocket that unwrapped to reveal an apple. He offered a slice to each woman, who declined. With a sneering bite of the fruit, he flicked the horses into motion. Along the gravel path, a great blue heron lifted off from the reeds with a harsh series of croaks as it faded into a silhouette.

13

WRITING HOME

It was Matthew who knelt before a large fire that popped and hissed as embers fluttered like flies about his head. Beside him, a small collection of the deserter's belongings remained. The cool blue hue of night was settling in, and the wind lifted off the water, drawing the flames upward with tugs. Matthew stood up with a newspaper in his hand, looked to it, then out at the river, and fed a page. Against the wall of the fort, his shadow flickered and shifted in a flashing silhouette.

Henry could make out the figure of Matthew between the brightness and the tailing shadows. Matthew stood again, throwing something else into the flames, then hunched back down. Henry whistled bobwhite as he approached, prompting Matthew to swing his head around and squint, unable to see.

"Who?" he said.

"Henry."

"Henry?" Matthew pivoted back to the fire. "Cowardly bastard. You up and leave—damned coward."

"I understand."

Henry met Matthew by placing a hand on his shoulder. Matthew turned to see Henry's face illuminated. The deep shadows that spread from his eyes amplified the stern look on his face.

"I'm sorry I left," Henry said. "I shouldn't of done that to you."

"Ha! To me? You miserable piece of shit. You no good miserable piece of shit!"

Henry hung his head, and it was only then that he located the deserter's belongings beside the cylindrical gleam of a bottle of wine lying on its side.

Matthew went on. "You're a deserter now, friend. Can't nobody save you. You'll be next on the gallows."

He began laughing in a rehearsed way. His chuckle rose into chirps until they tailed off with a sigh. Pointing, unsteady, he said, "Can't nobody save you from the gallows. You'll see. Another day—two days, and you'll be a-swinging in that fine summer breeze."

Henry exhaled and sat in the dirt beside the fire. He looked around, admiring how the darkness softened the landscape into inky layers.

"I couldn't do it, Matthew. I haven't got a clue how you did it, to be honest."

"I did what I had to do," Matthew said, teeth bared and pointing again. He stared off the tip of his index finger, then a smile broke over his face as he reached for the wine. "So, where'd you go? Where'd you head, you blasted coward? Where's a coward head when he steals a horse?"

Henry shook his head, spread the pile of the deserter's belongings with the toe of his boot. He took up an envelope that spilled from a small bag and held it before the fire. The writing on the letter within was revealed against the backdrop of the fire.

"I went north a few miles," he said. "Camped in a marsh."

Matthew put the bottle to his lips and a sound from deep inside hinted it was nearly empty. It squeaked away from his lips. He wound up and tossed it toward the water with an exaggerated motion. He rocked back and forth for a moment, eventually teetering over onto his back. Henry observed the behavior out of the corner of his eye as he tucked the letter back in the satchel.

"What are you burning here?"

"Trash from the spectacle. Flyers and tickets and the like. The wind collected them in the corner here."

Matthew began humming, sprawled out and waving his feet side to side. The soft melody broke into pieces as he began sobbing. He brought his hands to his head and pulled his hat over his face as he wept.

Henry grinned. "How much have you had to drink?"

He looked to the man as his chest rose and fell. Matthew began to gain control of himself and fell silent, hands still holding his hat over his face. Henry turned back to the fire with a shrug and began to read the flyers.

"I guess that's just the way it goes," he said. "They never even stopped to think that they'd have done the same thing in his shoes."

Matthew grabbed a large handful of cloth on Henry's shoulder and pulled himself back into a seated position.

"The scaffold held." He pulled Henry's face close to his. "That body swung, and the scaffold held."

Henry arched an eyebrow and nodded. Matthew pulled him closer before shoving him back.

"So, you're happy with your work, then?"

Matthew's eyes appeared transfixed by the light of the dancing flames, but his head bobbed in gentle response.

"Some service to the army you've provided," Henry said. "You're more a soldier than I'd hope to be, for sure."

Matthew dropped his head into his hands and his body shook. Henry began to pat him on the back, but Matthew rolled his shoulder away and stood up with a wobble. He paced away from the fire, and the night enveloped him. A moment later, he emerged again. The hard expression on his face resisted the light.

Henry rolled a flyer into a ball and placed it into the fire.

"I'll admit something," Matthew said. He took several deep, sobering breaths. "Yeah. I have something to admit."

He took quick, deliberate strides towards Henry, who flinched as Matthew moved past him to the deserter's belongings. He took up the old uniform and cast it into the flames. The wool charred and curled, and the black acrid smoke distilled the light to a glow.

Henry stood, dusting off the seat of his pants.

After staring at the leaping flames for a moment, Matthew spoke. "I built the scaffold—stuck to your plan. It held." He belched. "I couldn't have done it without you. Couldn't have."

Both men stood silent for a moment before the pillar of black smoke that swept the sky clean of stars.

"You were very helpful in hanging that man. The Union Army thanks you." Matthew saluted him and spat at his feet.

Henry contemplated the remaining belongings. "Like I said, you're a better soldier than I am, Matthew. I couldn't see it through to the end. I just couldn't do it."

Matthew began to laugh again, this time a soft muffled chuckle. Shaking his head, he said, "No. I couldn't do it either. You and your goddamn ideas—I couldn't do it either."

Henry offered no response. The charred linen of the uniform curled in on itself, and the fire faded low, raising a rank scent like burnt hair.

Matthew exhaled and inflated his cheeks. "No," he said, "I couldn't execute the son of a bitch."

"How's that?"

"When they noticed you'd gone, they picked me to do it." He drew out his words in a low voice. "And I couldn't do it."

Henry said nothing. Matthew looked at him with widened eyes, wanting to read his reaction.

"You happy, you damned deserter?" he added, prodding Henry's shoulder.

Again, Henry did not offer a response.

Matthew lunged and shoved Henry to the ground. The two men fought clumsily, Matthew attempting to hit Henry in the face, while Henry held him about the wrists. Henry rolled Matthew onto his side, and in one violent motion, tore himself free of the attacker.

Matthew was unsteady in taking to a knee, and Henry again shoved him down.

"It's not our fault!" he said, as Matthew flopped over.

Again, Matthew attempted to take to his feet, and again Henry shoved him back to the ground.

Henry took up the small pile of remaining flyers, and grabbing Matthew by the collar, he waved them in his face.

"They shouldn't have killed this poor bastard, and you know it. There isn't any shame in it. Look!" he said. "Tell me he didn't give enough! Now get up, you sorry bastard."

Matthew stood up and dusted himself off. The uniform in the fire was all but gone. Matthew reached for the satchel and moved to toss them into the flame. Henry tore it loose from his hands and shoved him back once more.

"I didn't run," Matthew said. "What kind of coward runs?"

"Matthew, I—"

"What kind of son of a bitch runs?" He spat and marched off.

Henry watched the open mouth of the fort swallow him up as the humming glow of the fire pit pulsed along the wall. He took up the satchel that had belonged to Howe. Among the few personal effects contained therein was the single letter. Taking it up again, he could see it was addressed to Howe's wife in the town of Perkiomenville.

Matthew returned with a small load of cord wood cradled in his arms. He dropped the wood and began to theorize on what would bring the war to an end. Using a straight branch, he poked at the embers releasing sparks that climbed on the thermal current of the flames.

Henry interrupted his commentary. "Where's Perkiomenville?"

"Damned if I know. Only thing I know is the Rebels will never make it that far North."

Henry drifted away from the conversation, took to his feet, donned the satchel and made his way to the horse.

The next morning the rising late summer sun condensed the night into heavy dew. Henry had ridden some twenty miles up the pike before stopping to sleep in a cleared spot where the road shouldered up against a large waterway. In the night, he had located the fire ring and gathered a small amount of sticks, but sleep caught up with him before he ever struck a match.

Now the streamside was awaking in song and minute activity. He heard the deep snort of his horse just before he felt a soft nudge against his leg.

"How now?" a man said, pressing his boot again against Henry's leg.

"Get the hell back," Henry said as he sat up.

"Now friend, let's calm down." The man was a fisherman, his round face encircled by the floppy brim of his weathered hat. His flies were hooked into its fabric haphazardly, as if they'd landed there on their own. Against the early wash of light, he appeared filthy, as if he'd lived his whole life on the streamside and never touched the water except to extract a caught fish.

"Mind if I make use of this fire pit here?"

Henry stood up and took in his surroundings for the first time. The area where he had bedded was a cleared section with a downed tree serving as a bench, the bark worn smooth, beside a soft promontory that overlooked a large open stretch of water know as the Perkiomen Creek. Sometime ago a traveler collected large stones into a ring, and the ashes of countless fires picked up like pollen in the wind.

Gaining his senses Henry said, "Just passing through. Pit's all yours." He made his way down to the water's edge to rinse his face and shock himself into a sharper sense of wakefulness.

The fisherman busied himself among the undergrowth, collecting kindling and striking up a small cook fire. He let out a sharp whistle shriek, and, gaining Henry's attention at the water, he pointed to where a stringer was knotted to an overhanging branch.

Once Henry washed his mind clear, he made his way to the line. The rainbow trout were tethered together in a cluster, flashing beneath the undulating golden sheen of the water. He lifted the fish out and laid them flopping wild in the lush grass on the bank. Amongst the stones and rubble, he found a sharp shard of slate which he used to pierce the flesh and clean the fish. The blood ran dark over his hands as he removed the organs. He dunked and rinsed the carcasses several times.

The fisherman was tending a stoutly constructed fire, with a stone placed in the middle, darkening.

"You've had some success along this stretch," Henry said.

"Here and there. I've given it some time."

"Do you live right around here?"

"Upstream a ways." The fisherman quickly tapped the flat stone. "Mind if I ask whereabouts you're headed?" He did not look up as he checked the condition of the trout.

"I'm a soldier—well, I've got a letter to deliver."

The fisherman only nodded as he placed the fish on the stone. Shaking his hands cool, he took a seat on the log.

Henry continued, "Not my letter. I'm just the courier."

"Ah." The fisherman closed his eyes and inhaled deeply. Upon opening his eyes and focused on Henry. "Whereabouts you headed?"

Henry stood and retrieved the satchel from the horse.

"I'm looking for a woman with the last name Howe. A German woman. Address is here." He handed the letter to the fisherman.

"Howe."

"That's right. I've come up from Fort Mifflin. I'd like to get this to his wife. Posthumous. Feels as though I owe him the service."

Notes from a Deserter

The fisherman handed Henry the letter and used a small stick to roll the trout over. He busied himself among his belongings and produced a small tin plate and an eating utensil. As he worked, his eyes peeked out from under the brim of his hat and appeared so light blue they hinted at a level of blindness.

"Only have the flatware for one," he said. "But you're welcome to some breakfast." He poked the trout with his fork. "Another minute or so." For a moment he sat and smiled at Henry, his plump cheeks forested by sun bleached white whiskers.

Henry thanked him, adding, "So, does the name ring a bell? Howe?"

The fisherman was quiet a moment. He cleared his throat. "I believe I do know a Howe. In fact, I saw him just yesterday."

"Yesterday? Not the same fellow."

"Oh, you see, it is the same fellow. I saw him yesterday, in the evening. He didn't have much to say though."

"I think we're talking about different men," Henry said.

"Supposed it could be, but not likely."

The trout sizzled against the stone. The fisherman stuck one with his fork and worked it loose on a stone beside Henry. He then propped the brim of his hat up with the utensil, his bright eyes flashed, and with an exhale of satisfaction he said, "Eat up."

Henry peeled the skin of the trout back and picked at the meat. "Where did you see—"

"How long were you in the army, then?"

"About a year I'd say."

"Seen some horrible scenes, I'd imagine."

"I'm luckier than most."

"How's that".

Henry ran his fingers along the inside of the fish's skin and collected a small hunk of meat. "I spent most of my time around the Fort. We would organize supplies for the wagons trains or fill box cars. Like that."

"But you were a soldier?"

"I was—but there were the other soldiers lived in camps and fought from time to time."

"Ah", said the fisherman. "You ever come across those types?"

"I did." Henry turned his fish around to work the meat out of the opposite side.

"And what were they like."

As he licked his fingers he said, "Damaged. Ruined. Just in bad shape. Drinking a lot at first to fight off the soldier's heart. They were emptied out, but at least they were going back home." Henry flung the papery carcass of the empty fish into the water.

"I'll say, you should've seen Howe." The fisherman had collected a pile of the fresh meat into the corner of his plate. Balancing it on his fork, he took a mighty bite.

"Yes—about Howe. Where is it you said you saw him?"

The fisherman smiled as he chewed, his eyebrows bunny hopped. After a great swallow he said, "He was in a box on a wagon full of shovels headed up the road. Nope, poor bastard didn't have much to say at all."

As he slowed his horse to a trot, Henry could see two men with two boys working along a stacked stone wall that separated a wood line from a field. The men drove shovels into the earth beside an impressive mound of misplaced soil while the boys removed and rolled any stones that had been excavated. It was nearing high noon, and the canopy shade had given way to the heat of the day. Dry dirt hung in the air in clouds, and the men ceased their work and stared as Henry approached.

The three adults exchanged tugs on the brims of their hats. Beside the sizeable hole, the sharp angles of a long wooden box contrasted the rolled edges of the stone wall. Meeting the edge of the wood lot, Henry could see a stone farmhouse squatting along the road with a few out-buildings scattered about.

As his horse came to stop Henry called, "Howe?"
"How what?"
"Sorry, sir. Is that Howe?"
"Is that how what?"
"William Howe."
"Where are you from?"

Henry squinted at the man, whose mouth flattened out as he leaned against the handle of his spade. His skin had cured into a dark leather complexion from the labor the land demanded during the growing and harvest seasons. They dug beside a massive granite boulder that served to mark where one property ended and another began. The boulder seemed bent over as if it were interested in their labor.

"I'm from Fort Mifflin. I've some belongings of Mr. Howe that I think his wife might want to have."

They stared at one another in a moment of silence. The man leaned his shovel against the stone wall and removed his gloves. "Jim, grab a pail of water from the well," he said pointing. "We'll take a half hour break, then get this finished up and done by sunset. Boys, go check the animal's water. Take the dog."

The other worker, a comparatively older man, did not hesitate and made his way to a patchwork of fields that spread out from that single stone farmhouse basking in the sun. As they wandered off, the other man approached Henry.

"You serve with Howe?" he asked.
"No, sir."
"Are you one of the cowards that killed this man?"
"No, sir." Henry shook his head with a slight pout to his lip. "I'm just the courier from Mifflin. I've got some of his belongings…"

He removed the satchel and held it out to the man

who snatched it away, taking several steps backward.

"What's your name?"

"Henry."

"Henry—my son's name is Henry. Nothing much but a letter?"

He handed it back to Henry, and again took a few steps back. He placed his hands on his hips and looked out toward the fields where Jim was pumping a well beneath a large black walnut tree.

"Well, honestly, she'll be happy to get that letter. Might take her some time to get around to reading it, but she'll be glad to have it."

Henry nodded. "Can I ask you something? They say this man fought well for the Union. Why bury him in a lawn up here? Why not—"

"The church over in Obelisk won't have him since he's convicted of deserting. Been dead a while—need to plant him soon." He paused and turned his face as a cool wind picked up. "He belongs here anyway," he added.

Staring at the house from a few hundred yards away, Henry could see a faint figure in the upstairs window. The windowpane itself flashed a bright diamond of sunlight, but behind that glassy reflection he was sure that a person was watching.

He turned to thank the man, but the man had already begun digging again and did not lift his head in response. The pit was waist deep and growing deeper with every stroke of the spade.

Henry dismounted his horse and strode along the road, tying the horse to the fencepost of a corral that housed two mules who took no interest in either of the visitors.

Looking up at the window from a short distance away, the window was no longer transparent; it held only the likeness of the sky within its frame, with heavy white clouds on a blue field. The canopy of the woodlot that the house was nestled in had begun the faint freckling of red and orange that was the first hint of fall.

The boys were now dropping large, recovered stones into the well, amused at deep echoes that rose in report. Seeing Henry approach the porch, they took up the pale of water and were off into the green and golden landscape. A small, wiry black dog trotted along with them.

Henry knocked on the door in a soft pattern, convinced that his arrival had been anticipated since he crossed the face of the granite boulder. Inside he heard the patter of young feet drum across the floor upstairs, but no sound motioned toward the door.

He noticed that there was enough firewood stacked to make it clear through to the next summer. The larger barn contained a wagon weighed down by crates of fresh picked fruits and vegetables; the fruit laden trees sagged their limbs beyond a lush field of corn. The two seemingly unaffectionate mules leaned their heads over the fence in the direction of the burial, appearing to wish to help in the work.

Three more knocks and Henry stepped off the porch, leaving Howe's pack resting beside the door. The whole place felt alive; the two boys climbed a distant fence as the wind picked up and instigated waves from the treetops to the fields of crops. Chickens called out and cackled at one another, the mules repositioned and stomped their feet, and Jim was returning to the burial with a pail of fresh water. Looking upward, vultures had caught the scent and sliced through the brilliant sunlight on high.

Henry entered into the barn and re-emerged with a shovel in hand and went off to help finish digging.

As Henry approached the men, neither one reacted to his arrival. He removed his coat. He rolled his sleeves and said, "Must of been a fine farmer." He took up his shovel and busied himself in the task of burying the deserter.

-The End-

Notes from the Author

A few years after my wife and I had purchased our little farmhouse in Perkiomenville, PA, a stranger pulled into the driveway while we were grilling for Mother's Day. I assumed she was asking directions, which was the case. However, what was unexpected that day in early May was that she was looking for directions to a nearby grave in the woods. At the time, I had no knowledge of a grave in the neighboring woodlot, but I was more than happy to risk getting poison ivy as we went poking around.

The grave in question, which is down the hill from our house, belonged to one William Henry Howe. Though we didn't find the gravestone on that Mother's Day, that random encounter started me on an interesting part-time obsession with the history of our little farmstead plot, in our little town, in the surrounding area of Philadelphia dating back to the year 1863.

In finding some cursory articles and one out-of-print book entitled *Stop the Evil,* a story fell into place that centered around a fateful night where a firefight took place near Howe's farmstead in Perkiomenville. By the end of that night, the previous owners of our farmhouse were busy moving the body of a fallen bounty hunter who had tried to follow through on a citizen's arrest of a deserter. Some six months later, after a trial and letters to Lincoln, despite a reputation for having fought bravely in the lopsided Battle of Fredericksburg, Howe was hanged for murder and desertion. His body was then buried on his property after having been rejected from the local graveyard in Obelisk, PA. His final resting place ended up being just off the road, marked by a small gravestone on a neighboring property.

Notes from a Deserter

❧

Throughout the research process, I read any Civil War piece I could find, visited battlefields, read PDFs of soldier's journals through the Library of Congress, and fell asleep in my kids' room with the iconic Ken Burns documentary on a virtual loop on my laptop. With every new narrative of each facet of the war, I was continually in awe of the cultural shifts that were forced upon the entire country of thirty-six states and territories in just a few short years. As I worked on the manuscript during grad school at Arcadia University, and then through the COVID pandemic, I came to appreciate the modern cultural shifts that can make the span of a few years seem like decades of change.

As I learned more about Howe and researched his specific desertion story, it became clearer that he likely had dysentery from living in squalid camps as the war dragged on. Clean drinking water was often hard to come by, and any food they could scavenge beyond hardtack (a mix of flour, salt, and water) was often rotten fruit. The oft-repeated Civil War fact remains true: the number one cause of death was diarrhea.

From the perspective of the individual, or specifically Howe, the great machinery of the army in the operation of war looks different. The Battle of Fredericksburg was an atrocity where Confederate lines held the high ground many days in advance of the Union charge. As the Union soldiers surged up the great fields of Marye's Heights, they fell in waves. Soldiers ducked from enemy fire atop the hill, but also had to fight through their dead and dying brethren who were sometimes pulling at their legs to discourage them from charging into certain death. It was a battle so gruesome that it resonated with Robert E. Lee, who commented afterward that, "It is well that war is so terrible, or we should grow too fond of it."

As the cold descended on the survivors at night, they

would sneak into the mass heap of the dead in the field to steal extra layers of clothing. When the sun rose the next morning, soldiers described the nude frozen corpses as resembling sheep afield. Somewhere in between that unholy flock and the ransacked town of Fredericksburg, William Howe was likely traumatized by what he had seen in battle and agonized by stomach pains from living in camps.

To this point, he hadn't received more than a few dollars for his service and understood the spring would bring a new baby and a fresh planting season hundreds of miles away in Perkiomenville. With medical facilities in both Virginia and D.C. being overrun, Howe made the obvious choice. One could imagine that he saw his duty as fulfilled, and with many of his commanding officers fleeing to Philadelphia to regroup, Howe decided to do the same. It is impossible to find the path that he took, but somehow, he found his way along the 275 miles that lay between him and his young family. He made a rather courageous decision to desert.

Earlier in my collegiate career, as an undergrad at the University of Montana, I fell in love with the work of Charlie Russell. Born in St. Louis at the tail end of the Civil War in 1864, Russell was a western painter who realized that the American West was a dynamic era subject to change. His works range from drawings on personal correspondence that are essentially cartoons of the going's-on of cowboy-life on the open range, to vibrant paintings that prominently display the nuance and detail of the indigenous cultures set against their historic backdrop of oceanic plains and fantastic skylines serrated by the Rocky Mountains. One piece that always stood out in my mind is his masterpiece titled "Lewis and Clark Meeting the Flathead Indians at Ross' Hole." I studied a reprint on a near daily basis which came to me as a graduation gift from my parents.

"Lewis and Clark Meeting the Flathead Indians at Ross's Hole" by Charlie Russell (1912)

In the portrait, the crisp blue sky is interrupted with energetic clouds that move from white to gray as they are forced upward into the Big Sky. It draws the eye into the distance, where the peaks dissipate into a purple haze. The Flathead subjects motion inward to the center of the painting in a flurry of activity. The individuals depicted rear up on some half dozen animated horses in the center, holding spears that protrude upward into the uneasy sky.

To the left of the central figures, a large congregation of teepees are naturally situated in the rolling prairies. To the right, the small figures of Lewis and Clark, along with Sacagawea and their interpreter, Toby, meet and converse through the shared language of sign. Canines lope through the grass, fog lifts from the foothills to join the building cloud cover, and a bighorn skull rests offset from the centralized activity. The scene is very much alive, no doubt fueled by Russell's own childhood curiosity of Lewis and Clark as he was told stories of their 1806 return by his great grandfather, Silas Bent, who bore witness firsthand to his own seismic American cultural shift. Bent was present in St. Louis when the Corps of Discovery made their triumphant return.

I mention the work of Charlie Russell for two major reasons, the first of which is that he inspired my continuing

Notes from the Author

love of American history. The drama and animation of his pieces amplify the tragedy and inspiration of the individuals who called themselves Americans as they worked to develop a clear conception of what it even meant to be American. "Lewis and Clark Meeting the Flathead Indians at Ross's Hole" stands out as a powerful piece of American iconography because of a specific choice that Russell made. The indigenous, in all their natural pageantry, steal the show, while the Corps of Discovery is a minuscule side note that one must intentionally pick out and bring into focus. Any mythology in the piece is reserved for the natives on horseback, an indication of Russell's advocacy for the indigenous peoples of the American West which, in part, helped lead to the establishment of the Rocky Boy Reservation in 1916.

Secondly, this specific piece serves as a reminder that all the major players in each historical era were and are human. Driven by the passion of ambition, duty, and cultural expectations, they raised families, built communities, and worked from day to day for what they saw as positive development. The same is true for the men and women in the divided country of the American Civil War, as they struggled to recalibrate what their cultural expectations were and would be moving forward. Indeed, it is the same now, as Americans are doing their best to be neighbors and parents, coworkers, and community members, in a country that *seems* like it is shifting beneath our feet more than ever.

In service of examining the ways in which the country shifted for the people of the 1860s, each section of the book is inspired in the Russellian way to examine one of those major flashpoint moments that signaled that our society would never be the same. The narrative of Howe, and how he came to his final resting place, is the unifying background feature. Similar to the Flathead and the landscape of Lolo, Montana, minimizing Lewis and Clark, I sought a sort of tilt shift to the narrative that unfolded as I followed the time period of Howe's day and age. The Civil War was originally expected to last only a few months. As it labored into its fifth year, every American from the enslaved to the enlisted knew that the experience of their children would be drastically different from the setting they had grown up in. Monumental change was on its way.

At the onset of the war, many eager, early volunteers signed ninety-day enlistment papers. As the war dragged on for years, the tides pushed and pulled participants in for a variety of reasons. Patriotism called the names of some enlistees, while others succumbed to simple peer pressure. Despite Lincoln's attempt to prohibit child soldiers (after initially approving child soldiers with parental consent), historians estimate some ten percent of the Union army consisted of individuals younger than fifteen. What would it be like for someone like Howe, buckling under social pressure, to arrive at an enlistment office and see a child with more conviction than some of the grown men in line? What would it be like for a woman to feel the calling and attempt to hide her gender through the enlistment process?

Perhaps what took the most mettle happened before a soldier ever left home, discussing leaving the wives and young mothers to tend a farm could not have been an easy conversation over a candlelit dinner. It was surely no easy task to convince their significant other that the risk was worth the reward. Victorian gender roles buckled under the stress of extraordinarily high male casualties as well as soldiers returning with PTSD, then known as *Soldier's Heart*. Women kept communities knitted together, not just through rearing the young while the fathers were away, but by taking over the daily operations of their farmsteads. In the absence of their husbands, they became the lynchpins of the family and communities alike. In an agricultural community such as Perkiomenville, women were suddenly rearing animals in addition to their children and planning plantings and harvesting in addition to keeping house.

Many "country boys", as Howe was called, had never ventured much further than their immediate local

Notes from the Author

communities. The wonders that awaited the enlisted were not limited to the various cities and states that they would visit by foot or by rail. It was during the Civil War that flight was first used in American battles, through hot air balloons being used as reconnaissance tools. The Balloon Corps was a fleet of seven hot air balloons that would stay tethered to the ground but could reach a height of 1,000 feet in order to gain a visual approximation of Confederate movements. To be a young person from any number of agricultural towns and witness a manned flight of such heights must have been an astounding and unforgettable experience. Though estimates pose that a soldier spent twenty-eight days idle for every one day of fighting, witnessing technological advances such as the aeronautics program and advancements in train technology could have been highlights of one's journey into the unknown.

The mass casualties of unnamed bodies that piled up in freshly churned battlefields changed the national perception of death, as well as the rituals applied to funerals. The prewar culture clung to Victorian standards of etiquette surrounding the death of a family member. Traditionally, the body would be displayed for three days so that extended family could travel to see the departed, paying homage and praying vigil. Ancestral portraits could be displayed, and sometimes a death portrait would be taken. In an era where photography was new technology, taking a photo of the recently-deceased was the last chance to preserve their likeness in a life where they likely hadn't had their image recorded by any other means.

As the war dragged on and the death toll mounted, anonymous bodies would be cleared from battlefields and deposited in mass graves. The funerary transition was underway as funerals stopped being private, in-home events, and now became public events at a local church where townsfolk could come and share condolences. Even Lincoln's own funeral was unique for its time. With rapid advancements in embalming, the president's corpse was treated for transport in the pre-refrigeration era which allowed for his corpse to be displayed along a 1,600-mile route aboard a train called *The Lincoln Special*. Through 400 cities and towns, mourners put their political parties aside to observe the body of the fallen President, including a rare photo of six-year-old Teddy Roosevelt at his grandfather's window watching as the procession made its way through New York City.

The new technology of photography introduced propagandistic photographs to show the brutality of war to the population at large. Intrepid photographers would descend on battlefields shortly after the fighting had subsided in order to have pliable subjects to move into more dramatic poses. From the photography of Mathew Brady to the poetry of Walt Whitman to the increasingly more sophisticated political cartoons in *Harper's Weekly*, art would spring up from these most gruesome battles and raise the American discourse regarding the war.

The most important topic in the national discourse revolved around the enslaved Americans fighting for their own freedom. They were themselves a railroad, an army, a colony within the United States waging their own American Revolution. Some 180,000 black Americans freed by the *Emancipation Proclamation* immediately enlisted. Both runaway enslaved Americans and deserters were on foot, running below the fog of war along our great rivers and streams, migrating their way North.

Columns of soldiers marched like strings of ants across the landscape and the increased utility of the rail was about to usher in a golden age. Rail would soon firmly connect distant points of the country from north to south, as well east to west with the completion of the transcontinental railroad (1863-1869). The country was divided politically, but these seismic events that were happening at the foundational cultural levels were a convergent boundary; tectonic cultural plates were driving themselves into one another and a new American cultural landscape was emerging.

Notes from the Author

As a deserter after the Battle of Fredericksburg, Howe picked his way north and the societal changes rose ahead of him like the Rocky Mountains before Charlie Russell. He likely was sick with dysentery and unable to find medical care that wasn't overwhelmed with severe wartime injuries. Despite the ill-state he found himself in, he was able to cover 275 miles in his hidden walk. It is estimated that he returned home just before the birth of his second child, only to be arrested after a late-night firefight which resulted in the death of a bounty hunter. He would once again be taken from his family with no certainty of returning.

At Fort Mifflin, on August 26th, 1864, Howe shared his final words from the gallows. He began by offering forgiveness to those who sentenced him, stating, "[I] fully forgive those who passed [my sentence] and all who were witnessed against me. They did their duty as well as they could, and I take this opportunity to thank you from my heart...And now I am about to leave this life and I commend my wife and little ones to the charity of the world, and as a last request I ask pardon of those I injured and hope they will forgive me and pray for my soul." Shortly thereafter, despite letters on his behalf from his battalion and questionable evidence of his guilt, William Henry Howe became the first deserter to be made an example of. He was hanged and pronounced dead by a "dislocation of the neck."

Visitors to Fort Mifflin today can see his initials carved into the jail cell that held him within view of the gallows that were constructed to hang him before a crowd. Local lore posits that Howe is the "faceless man" that haunts Mud Island; faceless due to the bag that was placed over his head as the only deserted hanged at the fort during the war. Back home in Perkiomenville, his physical body was rejected from the local graveyard in Obelisk, PA, for fear of being associated with anti-war sentiment. His body made it home for good at last to be buried not far off the roadside on the little plot of land that he worked so hard to get back to.

Notes from a Deserter

Howe was a second-generation immigrant struggling to fit into his generation's perspective of the American Identity, which resulted in a series of large risks. The culture of his period offered him and millions of his generation a risk-reward proposition that carried social clout for them and resulted in liberty for unknown others. For a brief time, he rode the swift current of change that flooded his time period, but his misfortune was that there was a significant undertow. In the end, the story of William Henry Howe, interwoven into the broader tapestry of the American Civil War, is a reminder of the complexities and nuanced experiences that Americans faced in an era of ubiquitous transformation.

The Civil War was not merely a clash of armies peopled by countless unknowable soldiers, but an immeasurable tectonic shift that transformed the American landscape, both physically and culturally. Through the immersive experience of researching this narrative, the personal stories of soldiers like Howe bring to light the immense pressures faced by individuals caught in a whirlwind of historical change. Howe's desertion and subsequent execution underscore the harsh realities of the time, where there was tension between loyalty and survival, and where personal decisions weighed against the needs of the government which lead to severe consequences.

Drawing parallels to the works of Charlie Russell, who captured the dynamic transformative nature of the America West, Howe's story is a testament to the culture shifts instigated by the Civil War. Just as Russell's paintings juxtapose the grandeur of indigenous life against the encroaching forces of change, Howe's life represents the struggle of the individual against the forces of national upheaval. The war's impact on the familial roles, community structures, scientific limits, and personal identities was profound, reshaping the American ethos in lasting ways.

This analysis explored through the lens of a personal quest for historical understanding also serves as a bridge

Notes from the Author

to the contemporary American experience. The seismic shifts of the Civil War find echoes in today's rapid cultural and societal shifts. Just as the war forced Americans to redefine their national identity and community roles, modern society grapples with its own challenges of change. These many facets were funneled into a word document as I typed away not 200 yards from Howe's grave, sometime between the beginning of the COVID Pandemic and the notorious election of 2020.

    Howe's life and legacy, complicated though it may be, offers a window into the enduring human spirit amidst the trials of war. His story is interesting and special in its own right, but it is not entirely unique to the lived experience of countless Americans of his era. It is etched into the landscape of Perkiomenville and the annals of Civil War history as a reminder of the personal costs of national conflict in the relentless march of progress. By uncovering and sharing this story, I have found a deep appreciation for the complexities of the past, and the resilience required at the personal level to navigate the ever-changing currents of history using something as simple as the desire to be with one's family as a lodestar throughout the journey.

Acknowledgments

One of my hobbies on the farmstead uphill from Howe's grave is beekeeping. The interesting thing about the keeping of bees, besides seeing every stitch of your local environment, is that you cannot do it alone. In one sense, it is an individual moving the boxes and checking the frames and observing the behavior of the hive. However, that one person is going to have more success with their hives if they are tapped into their community of local beekeepers. The know-how, troubleshooting, excess supplies, and communal knowledge are invaluable. Through working on this book, I have learned that writing works the same way. You can only do it by yourself, but you could never do it *alone*.

My wife Justine kind of always knew I would write a book. She is such a patient spouse that she would not only let me wander off from a Mother's Day barbecue to go and look for a grave, but she supported and tolerated many historical obsessions that came along with the research. Further still, she loves to see that there is a genetic component to it, as our two sons have their own historical obsessions that they seek out in the nearly thirty-million acres of Penn's Woods. My bookish and crafty family raise the bar of what it means to take a project on. They are detail-oriented craftspeople and encouraged me as I took the long route to find mine. My in-laws read some early stories and celebrated each little step along the way and made it seem like Justine was right; I would get the book done at some point.

The MFA program at Arcadia University gave me an amazing experience from Pennsylvania to Edinburgh, but more importantly it intertwined my journey with the likes of Maddie Anthes, Nate Drenner, Nick Gregorio, Andy Mark, and Greg Oldfield. They are great writers, creative people, and took a lot of time to work through early versions of these chapters. Prof Isard and Prof Elwork welcomed me into a diverse and expanding community of writers that produces quality books of all shapes and sizes.

Lastly, I am a teacher. The youngest learners and the oldest educators have inspired me to keep working on my craft in little ways throughout my career. When I started working with the great team at History Through Fiction and realized this book would become a reality, my first thought was that if these young people see that I can do it, they will know that they can do it, too. So, get writing.

However this book came to you, thank you for reading.

– Chad Towarnicki

About the Author

C. W. Towarnicki is a father, writer, and educator living in Perkiomenville, PA. He holds an MFA from Arcadia University where he began drafting his first novel following a research subject, William Henry Howe, who left a neighboring property to enlist in the Civil War. He writes historical fiction short stories as well as nonfiction articles in the field of education. His work appears in *Education Weekly, Sundial Magazine, Fly Culture Magazine* and others. He is currently working on his second novel which is set to focus on the Pennsylvania Lumber Era of the late 1800s. He and his wife are founders of a Learner-Driven School called Seeds Academy in Green Lane, PA.

About HTF Publishing

Founded in 2023 as an imprint of History Through Fiction, HTF Publishing is hybrid publisher of compelling, high-quality historical novels. Following in the tradition of History Through Fiction, HTF Publishing seeks to provide readers with engaging historical narratives that are rooted in detailed and accurate historical research. As a hybrid press, we want to work with authors who are serious about their craft and aspire to share imaginative, important, and well-researched, historical narratives with the world.

If you enjoyed this novel, please consider leaving a review. It's the best way to support us and our authors. Plus, you'll be helping other readers discover this great story.

Thank you!

www.HistoryThroughFiction.com